"So here goes, folks. I'm going to propose. What I want is you, Hetty King. Will you marry me?"

Hetty closed her eyes. Dear Lord, she prayed, let me wake up from this terrible dream.

The voice came again. "What say we get hooked, poopsie," it insisted. "You know, hitched?"

She could feel him fumbling for something in his pocket. A loud gasp from the crowd forced her to peek. Wally had produced a small velvet box. Snapping it open, he drew forth a ring. He held it up for the crowd to admire. There were stones set in the ring. They looked like good stones. Like all good stones, they caught the sun's rays and played with them, throwing them up in the air, juggling with them.

Hetty's eyes open wider. Wally was holding the ring out to her. She looked up at him. Tears glistened in his eyes. His face came closer and closer. It looked solemn and happy. His arms encircled her, drawing her tightly to him. She could see the little red hairs in his moustache. Funny, she had never noticed how they matched the little red veins in his eyes. She could see his mouth. It hovered above hers. It kissed hers. The crowd broke into applause. At that moment Hetty woke from her frozen trance and pulled away from him violently.

"No! No!" she screamed. "Get away from me, you harebrained crackpot! I'll never marry you!"

**Also available in the Road to Avonlea Series
from Bantam Skylark books**

The Journey Begins
The Story Girl Earns Her Name
Song of the Night
The Materializing of Duncan McTavish
Quarantine at Alexander Abraham's
Conversions
Aunt Abigail's Beau
Malcolm and the Baby
Felicity's Challenge
The Hope Chest of Arabella King
Nothing Endures but Change
Sara's Homecoming
Aunt Hetty's Ordeal
Of Corsets and Secrets and True, True Love
Old Quarrels, Old Love
Family Rivalry
May the Best Man Win
Dreamer of Dreams
It's Just a Stage
Misfits and Miracles
The Ties That Bind
Felix and Blackie
But When She Was Bad...
Double Trouble
A Dark and Stormy Night
Friends and Relations
Vows of Silence
The Calamitous Courting of Hetty King

The Calamitous Courting of Hetty King

Storybook written by

Fiona McHugh

Based on the Sullivan Films Production
written by Fiona McHugh
adapted from the novels of

Lucy Maud Montgomery

A BANTAM SKYLARK BOOK®
NEW YORK · TORONTO · LONDON · SYDNEY · AUCKLAND

Based on the Sullivan Films Production produced by Sullivan Films Inc.
in association with CBC and the Disney Channel with the participation
of Telefilm Canada adapted from Lucy Maud Montgomery's novels.

Teleplay written by Fiona McHugh
Copyright © 1991 by Sullivan Films Distribution, Inc.

This edition contains the complete text
of the original edition.
NOT ONE WORD HAS BEEN OMITTED.

RL 6, 008–012

THE CALAMITOUS COURTING OF HETTY KING
A Bantam Skylark Book / published by arrangement with
HarperCollins Publishers Ltd.

PUBLISHING HISTORY
HarperCollins edition published 1995
Bantam edition / May 1995

ROAD TO AVONLEA is the trademark of Sullivan Films Inc.

Skylark Books is a registered trademark of Bantam Books,
a division of Bantam Doubleday Dell Publishing Group, Inc.
Registered in U.S. Patent and Trademark Office and elsewhere.

ISBN 0-553-48127-4

Bantam Books are published by Bantam Books, a division of Bantam Doubleday Dell
Publishing Group, Inc. Its trademark, consisting of the words "Bantam Books" and the
portrayal of a rooster, is Registered in U.S. Patent and Trademark Office and in other
countries. Marca Registrada. Bantam Books, 1540 Broadway, New York, New York 10036.

PRINTED IN THE UNITED STATES OF AMERICA
OPM 0 9 8 7 6 5 4 3 2 1

Chapter One

"Tootsies are big, dilly-dilly,
Tootsies are small ..."

Wally Higgens closed his eyes, opened his mouth and hurled his voice at the defenseless sky. Singing was his passion. Singing was almost as much fun as selling skates.

"... But size six tootsie-woo-ootsies
Are best of all."

Wally Higgens made a good salesman, but an appalling singer. Even his own mother would have admitted that his voice lacked charm. It rose now, sharp as a tack, scratching the shiny surface of the bright, winter day.

"I've searched the land, dilly-dilly,
Searched till I'm blind.
But no size six tootsie-woo-ootsies
Did I once find."

Making up little songs—or ditties, as he liked to call
them—seemed to Wally Higgens one of the best things
a fellow could do with his spare time.

Not that he had huge amounts of spare time himself.
No siree. His job as a skate salesman kept him constantly
on his toes, in a manner of speaking, moving up and
down the entire eastern seaboard. Still, traveling from one
small town to another could be mighty tiresome, especially in the dead of winter. Why, if a man didn't keep his
little gray cells in shape, he might just end up dying of
boredom. And he'd been fighting boredom ever since this
morning, when he'd left that one-horse burg after breakfast, a town so small it didn't even merit a name. That was
why he had to keep singing. If he didn't sing, he might
fall asleep right there on the buggy. His horse, Bumbles,
would bumble into a snowbank and there they both
might sit, till the crack of doom, frozen solid.

So here we go, thought Wally, tapping his cold feet
on the buggy floor to warm them, giving the reins a
little jingle. How's about another ditty? Something to
do with noses, this time. Mine feels like it's gonna fall
off from frostbite. How's about, "When your nose ...
dum de dum ..." Clearing his throat, he croaked:

*"When your nose turns blue
And your feet feel dead
An' all you can think of is your nice, warm bed ...
Then hurry, hurry do,
Before it's too late,
Hurry to the ice
For a fun-filled—Heavens to Betsy!!! Ayyyyy!"*

Wally had really meant to say "skate," but just as his tongue was forming one of his favorite words, an army of children on sleds had careened around the corner. One of them slammed into a snowbank almost directly in front of Wally's buggy.

With a whinny of protest, Bumbles reared up, her hooves narrowly missing several children. Before Wally could so much as yell "Whoa, hold on there!" she had taken to her heels, swerving and slipping in the snow.

"Now wait a second, Bumbles! Easy does it!" pleaded Wally, grasping the sides of the buggy. But Bumbles paid him no heed. Lifting her head and tossing her mane, she galloped faster and faster, feeling her load lighten as, one by one, her master's sample cases went sliding off into the lane. As she rounded a corner, the buggy banged against a snow-covered fence. Bumbles stumbled on, unaware that the impact had thrown the last of her load, her master, Wally Higgens, flat on his face into the snow.

The children raced around the curve in the lane and came to an abrupt halt.

"Oh cripes! Now we've done it!" gasped Felix. "He's dead!"

Gus Pike, running close behind Felix, swerved to one side and stopped. He gazed down at the man lying still in the snow. "He ain't movin', that's for sure," he said slowly, trying to catch his breath. He could feel fear flooding into him like the sea.

The children had run after the panicked horse as fast as their legs could carry them. The idea that their morning of fun might have caused an accident seemed hard enough to contemplate. The thought that they might have caused someone's death made their hearts almost stop.

"It's all my fault!" wailed Sara. "I was going much too fast on that sled. I'll never forgive myself!"

Felicity gulped. The man lay on his stomach, his arms outstretched. The back of his head did not look familiar. Nor did his clothes. Perhaps he was a stranger to Avonlea. A round, gray hat, of the type favored by businessmen, had rolled to the side of the lane. Wooden crates dotted the snow about him. His horse seemed to have disappeared.

"Just think, a stranger to Avonlea. And we treat him like this!" Felicity groaned. "Now he'll never come back."

"You wouldn't want a dead man coming back anyway," objected Felix, who, being a normal eleven-year-old boy, had an interest in everything gory and macabre. "You'd be the first to complain if he did. 'Specially if his neck was broke. Or his face all bloody."

"Is his face bloody?" whispered his ten-year-old sister, Cecily, stepping back immediately.

"Shouldn't we find out who he is—I mean—was?" asked Sara.

"We're not going to touch him, are we?" Cecily was on the verge of tears. "It's not right to touch dead people. Certainly not dead strangers."

"Somebody should take his pulse," said Felicity, with sudden resolution, although her feet felt weighted to the ground. "Otherwise we won't know if he really is dead or not."

Felix squared his shoulders, determined not to appear frightened. "His pulse? Sure, I'll take it! Let me take it!"

Nobody else moved. All eyes were riveted on the quiet, brown-coated form in the snow.

Feeling suddenly grown up, Felix knelt down beside the outstretched figure. His hand hovered over the man's fur collar. Then it moved down to his shoes, then back to his head. Finally he looked up at the others. His tone was aggrieved. "Don't just stand there," he snapped. "Tell me what the heck a pulse is! Where is it? And how do I take it?"

Just at that moment a voice spoke from beneath them. It was a deep voice, with a chuckle buried in it. "Now hold on, there!" it said. "I believe the ol' ticker's still pumpin'. Let me check. Why, yes. Yes, indeed it is."

As the children watched, open-mouthed, the dead stranger rose jerkily to his feet. "Anybody seen my specs?" he asked. His round face was wet with snow, his pale eyelashes fringed with white. "Gotta find them specs." Grunting, he bent down, patting blindly about by his boots.

An odd sound reached the children's ears. At first they thought the stranger was moaning in pain, still suffering perhaps from the effects of his accident. Then they realized he *was singing*.

"Roses are red," he groaned. "Violets are blue. But without my specs, I can't see their hue."

Chapter Two

Although the day had started out crisp and sparkling, by noon clouds had rolled in from the sea, covering up the blue sky and darkening the mood of the ladies who frequented Lawson's general store.

Rachel Lynde found herself remembering just how little she liked the incessant chatter of Mrs. Potts. Mrs. Potts wondered silently how a woman Mrs. Bugle's size could possibly wear such a preposterous hat. Eulalie Bugle's mind was so filled with a pressing, private problem of her own that she sat mute, barely able to think at all, while inside her purse, wrapped in a sheet of newspaper, part of her problem lay hidden. Elvira Lawson, standing behind her counter, wished they would all just go away and let her get on with her work.

As if sensing Mrs. Lawson's impatience, Rachel Lynde reached for her basket.

"I'll be running along home, then," she sighed. "The dinner won't cook itself."

Mrs. Potts and Mrs. Bugle rose too. But instead of advancing towards the door along with the other women, Mrs. Bugle took a step backwards, melting into the shadowy recesses of the store. There, hidden in the dark amongst the shelves, she accomplished the task she had set herself the night before. Then she reappeared into the light.

No one had noticed her absence, for all eyes were on the large window that fronted onto the street. Voices and hurried footsteps had arrested the women's attention. Before they could walk outside to investigate, the door burst open and the sun walked in, escorted by Sara and Felicity. At least, fanciful though it sounds, that's how it struck both Rachel and Eulalie at the time. The gloomy store suddenly filled with light, a light that seemed to originate in the infectious smile of a small, plump man with a comical red mustache, who now stepped forward. As he took Rachel's hand in his, the light reflected off his thick glasses, almost dazzling her.

"Walter Higgens is the name, " he beamed, his grip firm on her hand. "Skates are the game."

Rachel blinked. But Mr. Higgens had moved on and was shaking the hand of each lady in the store in turn. Rachel turned the information over in her mind. *Skates are the game*. What could he possibly mean?

"Walter Higgens, salesman," the stranger repeated now to the room in general. "From the Windy City Skate Company, home of the newly patented boot skate."

For a moment he paused, making sure the eyes of the assembled company were fixed on him. Then, straightening his back, he gave a little leap into the air, landing with his right foot extended on its heel, his hands forward, palms lifted upwards like a tap dancer. He had practiced this position in front of boarding house mirrors up and down the coast. He knew it to be the most effective way to deliver his best ditty, the one he had spent four whole weeks exercising his little gray cells on. His glasses twinkled. Opening his mouth, he recited:

> *"When things are turning glum,*
> *Get off your derrière.*
> *Take your sweetie skating,*
> *Feel a whole lot merr-ier."*

Rachel gasped at this startling use of a vulgar anatomical term in public—saying it in French did not make it any more polite. The giggles of Mrs. Bugle and Mrs. Potts, however, combined with Elvira Lawson's applause, covered whatever disapproval might have shown on Rachel's face.

"You like it?" Mr. Higgens was asking Elvira. "I made it up myself. With every pair of skates you purchase, you get a copy signed by yours truly."

"I'm sure you'll sell many skates this time of year,

Mr. Higgens," Elvira Lawson replied. "Avonlea's winter festival takes place next week, and skating's one of its main attractions. We'll certainly order a batch for the store."

Clara Potts moved quickly back to her seat. She too had noticed how the dreary day had suddenly brightened with the arrival of Wally Higgens. "As a matter of fact," she said, "I think I need a new pair of skates myself. Yes, indeed I do. This very minute." Her plump fingers scrabbled at her laced-up boots.

"Why, land's sake. So do I," declared Mrs. Bugle, easing her weight back into a chair as fast as she could. As far as she was concerned, anything was better than returning home. At home, where her husband's snores echoed through a house made empty by her daughter's departure, her problem always seemed worse. As soon as she walked in the door, it would rise up, from the corner in her mind where it crouched, and torment her.

Even Rachel put down her basket and thought about staying a little longer.

Only Felicity King seemed anxious to be gone. Bending, she placed the sample case she and Sara had helped carry into the store beside Mr. Higgens. Before he could launch into his sales pitch, she stretched out her hand.

"I'm afraid Sara and I must be going, Mr. Higgens," she said politely. "We're truly sorry about the accident. I'm sure the ladies here will take good care of you until Gus fetches your buggy. Come along, Sara." Taking Sara firmly by the hand, she left the store.

"Accident? Why, mercy me, what on earth do you mean?" gasped Clara Potts, wrenching her boots off her feet.

"You had an accident in Avonlea?" asked Rachel, wondering how such an important event could possibly have escaped her attention.

As Mr. Higgens pulled skate after skate out of his sample bag, he described his accident in the most amusing fashion, blaming no one and making no complaints.

He was, thought Rachel, one of the most agreeable men she had ever encountered. Not that she had encountered many agreeable men. Quite the contrary. Rachel had always declared that, faced with a choice between men and budgies, she would always favor the birds. Yet watching Mr. Higgens measuring Mrs. Potts's pudgy foot, listening to his entertaining chatter, she began to feel an irresistible desire for skates herself.

"I hope you'll forgive the state of my old boots, Mr. Higgens," said Clara Potts with a blush, doing her best to push the offending objects out of sight under her chair.

"Never apologize for old friends, ma'am," replied the salesman. "Old friends are best. King James always preferred his old shoes, remember? They were easiest on his feet."

"Go on with you, Mr. Higgens!" broke in Eulalie Bugle, a smile relieving her gloomy face. "You're only saying that to cheer us up. I'll bet you have Mrs. Higgens in stitches!"

Mr. Higgens's sunny face clouded over. "Sad to say, there is no Mrs. Higgens, ma'am."

Mrs. Potts was so surprised that her foot, which had been poised in the air to try on the skate, came thundering to the floor. As if in sympathy, Eulalie Bugle's jaw dropped too, all its chins a-wobble. It was as though an invisible thread attached to the spines of the four women had suddenly tightened. Jerking themselves upright, they gazed at Mr. Higgens with heightened interest.

"Why, the poor soul," whispered Elvira, lowering her voice out of respect. "Did she pass on recently, Mr. Higgens?"

"Well if she did, she must've passed right on by me," he replied, attempting, as he often did, to make a joke out of whatever made him unhappy.

"You mean, you're a bachelor? A catch like you?" demanded Mrs. Bugle incredulously.

"Not by choice, I assure you," answered Wally, unsure how to interpret this sudden interest in his marital status. "To tell you the truth, I've never found the right little woman for this particular travelin' man. No, no, ladies. Let me tell you, if I had my own way, I'd like nothing better than to settle down in wedded bliss in some nice little burg like Avonlea."

While Mr. Higgens's attention was taken up with Clara Potts, Rachel had unbuttoned both boots and slipped them off under her skirt. Now, her mind on Mr. Higgens's last remark, she grabbed the nearest skate available, a dainty little black creation, and attempted to pull it onto her foot.

"Well you've come to the right place if you've got matrimony on your mind, Mr. Higgens," she grunted, squashing her toes into the small opening. "Why, we've got more widows and spinsters in Avonlea than a cat's got whiskers."

But Mr. Higgens seemed not to have heard the good news. His eyes were riveted on Rachel's foot as it crushed the little skate under its weight.

"No! No, not that one!" he gasped, grabbing the skate from Rachel and holding it tenderly to him. "This one's not for sale, ma'am. I'm sorry, but it's ... Well, you see, it's kind of a good luck charm. "

"Pretty small charm, if you ask me," replied Rachel, nettled by his sudden grab. "What size is it anyway?"

Into Mr. Higgens's eyes crept a dreamy look. "Size six, quad A," he breathed. "The perfect skate for the perfect little feminine tootsie."

"Looks more like a doll's skate than a grown woman's," snapped Rachel.

"Oh, they're made to fit a woman all right. But in all these years and in all my travels, I've never found the perfect tootsie-wootsie to fit this skate." Wally's voice had grown soft and yearning. "But you know something, ma'am?" His wistful eyes looked straight into Rachel's. "When I find the woman who fits this skate, I'll have found the woman of my dreams."

Rachel's knees felt suddenly weak. "Gracious

Providence. What a romantic notion, Mr. Higgens," she replied faintly. "Imagine falling in love with a girl for her feet! Of all things!"

Wally stood up. It was clear that Rachel had tapped deep into the wellspring of his most sacred beliefs. "Feet, my dear lady, are one of the great mysteries of life. Show me your feet, say I, and I'll show you your character."

As though with one accord, the three women raised their stockinged feet.

"Wait! Wait for me!" screamed Elvira, rushing from behind the counter, kicking off her boots as she went. She plopped herself down beside Rachel.

Wally Higgens looked down at the four pairs of feet raised up to him for inspection.

"Well, go on," challenged Rachel. "Show us our character."

"It really is all there, in the feet, ladies, waiting to be read. The rise of the arch, the length of the toes, the shape of the heel ..." He felt suddenly nervous. What if he said the wrong thing? Misinterpreted an arch, say? Would these nice ladies turn on him? Run him out of town?

"So what are you waiting for?" Mrs. Bugle's chins quivered with impatience. Perhaps this man had been sent to help her. Perhaps, somehow, he would remove the terrible burden from her shoulders. "Read my feet."

Off we go, thought Wally, in for a penny, in for a pound.

Clara Potts's foot was nearest to him. He reached over and studied it. "All right, then," he began. "Take this arch, for instance. See? Nice and high, so it is. That shows an artistic sensibility."

Mrs. Potts glowed. No one, absolutely no one, had ever before suggested that she harbored an artistic sensibility. She sat back, clutching her suddenly precious foot, while a whole new realm of possibilities opened before her eyes. Perhaps she should acquire one of those three-legged gizmos. What were they called now, easels? And one of those hats with the huge, floppy brims? Anne Shirley had worn one once, she remembered, and though she had sneered at her for wearing it, she had to admit it looked most becoming. Yes, she would wear exactly such a hat, sitting outside under the shade of the old plum tree. Plum trees were artistic. An easel, a floppy hat, a plum tree—they all added up. But to what? Why, to painting, of course! That was it. She would become a painter. But what in tarnation could she paint? Visions of her husband's pigpen floated into mind. After all, you couldn't sit under that plum tree and not notice the pigpen. It was the main feature of the place, really. But would anyone buy such a painting? she wondered, her spirits suddenly drooping. Of course, foreigners would, people from away. After all, not everyone was lucky enough to own a pigpen. There must even be some unfortunates who might live out their whole lives without ever coming into contact with one. Such people would be thrilled to find the genuine article recreated on canvas. They would hang it on their living room walls. All their friends would envy them. These friends would write to Clara, begging her to send them just such a work of art. She would grow famous, and rich, too. Her name would be featured in the Charlottetown Gazette. Now, if only she could figure out what to do about her signature. Potts sounded so, well, so unartistic, quite frankly. Perhaps she could slip an "e" in somewhere, or a "y"?

Unaware of the impact of his interpretation on Mrs. Potts, Wally had moved on to Rachel.

"These even toes here, see?" he said, running his index finger along Rachel's left foot. "Now they're the trait of a straight-shooter, if ever I saw one. One look and you can tell. These toes belong to a person who is honest as the day is long."

Rachel almost burst with pride. Why, here at last was someone who understood her to her very core. She was a straight-shooter. Didn't she pride herself on always speaking her mind? And if she occasionally hurt someone's feelings or caused a row, was that her fault? Was she to suppress one of her finest instincts merely from fear of causing offence? Not Rachel Lynde. No, she would be forever true to her nature. Her heart swelled. Yes, better to die on one's feet, especially if they were straight-toed, than live on one's knees.

Wally moved on to Mrs. Bugle. Lifting one heavy foot in his hand, he paused.

She eyed him sharply. "Well, go on, man. Don't keep a body waiting like that." She felt all a-tremble. So much so that she had to prop her raised leg up with both hands, to prevent its shaking from showing. She hoped the other women would not notice.

Wally could tell at one glance those tootsie-wootsies spelled trouble. Under streaky black stockings the toes clenched and dipped like miniature hillocks. He took a deep breath, feeling rather like a young soldier wading into his first battle.

"Well now," he said bravely, "I see here you've got your corns and your calluses and other, well, disruptions." He hesitated.

In the silence he could hear Mrs. Bugle's breathing. It seemed tense, labored. He could feel through her foot the shaking of her whole body.

"I can see for myself I have corns and calluses, Mr. Higgens. What do they mean? That's what I want you to tell me."

"Honesty is the best policy, remember, Mr. Higgens," piped up Rachel, who had caught his look of panic as he first took hold of Eulalie's foot. "Take it from one who knows."

Wally's genial face looked somber. "I'm afraid they mean a pinched personality, ma'am," he said finally. "Seems to me your life is full of worry and woe. "

Eulalie Bugle's small eyes filled with tears. "Amen to that, Mr. Higgens," she said softly. Pulling her feet away, she began stuffing them back into her dilapidated boots.

No one spoke. The radiant atmosphere that had suffused the store seemed dispelled.

Rachel broke the awkward silence. "To tell you the God's truth—which you can always rely on me to do, Mr. Higgens—I never thought of feet in that way before. I was brought up not to mention my feet at all."

Wally Higgens looked at the three faces turned up to him, and the fourth turned away.

"Always respect your feet, ladies," he replied solemnly. "They are a window to the soul."

Clara Potts stirred in her seat. "I really must go and study our pigpen before the light fails," she said mysteriously. Pulling the knots tight on her boots, she stood up. "Perhaps by tomorrow, you'll have found my size in skates, Mr. Higgens. I'll try to fit you into my schedule then."

There was an element of pity in her glance as she surveyed the others. "I, for one, can't afford to waste any more of today on fripperies. You know how it is, Mr. Higgens. We creative people mustn't squander our God-given talents."

Outside, the clip-clop of Bumble's heels reminded Wally of a round of calls still to be made that day.

"If you'll excuse me, ladies," he said, picking up his coat, "I'll say my goodbyes now too. But never fear, I shall return."

Like the sun, Rachel wanted to add, but didn't. She smiled instead, so warmly that Wally, despite the shock of his accident and the niggling fear that he had wounded Mrs. Bugle's feelings, felt his spirits lift. Perhaps he might enjoy this business trip to Avonlea after all. Perhaps he might make some friends here. Perhaps—

and here his heart quickened—he might even meet the woman of his dreams.

Had Wally known what calamity awaited him in Avonlea, he would have fled from that town as though from a plague. Instead, he drove, whistling, over to Mrs. Biggins's boarding house, where he rented a room for the week.

Chapter Three

With the exception of her cousin Sara, no one in the Avonlea general store had noticed Felicity's anxiety to leave; they were all too distracted by the arrival of Mr. Higgens. But for some time Felicity's behavior had been such that anyone paying attention could have seen her mind was absorbed by a question all the more weighty for being unspoken. Twice in the past week she had let the bread burn. On Sunday she had gone to church in her second-best dress, an event that seriously alarmed her mother. Yesterday she had forgotten to add flour to the cake she was baking, resulting in a soggy mess that even Felix had refused to eat.

"Give it to the pigs," he had said indignantly. "It's pig swill, ain't it?"

He'd waited for Felicity to throw a temper tantrum, or, at the very least, correct his English, for she hated him to say "ain't." But Felicity had merely stood behind him, staring down at the brown puddle of a cake, which spread over his plate like a reproach. Then, without a word, she'd lifted the plate, opened the dresser drawer and dropped it inside. Still silent, she'd taken her sewing and left the room.

"Mercy me!" her mother had sighed, getting up from the table to rescue her dirty china from the drawer. "I don't know what ails that girl. A scorching hot cup of ginger tea before bed tonight, that's what she needs. Fetch the rest of the dishes, Felix. It's your turn to wash them."

Her father had said nothing. Pushing his chair back from the dinner table, he'd patted his pockets, looking for his pipe. He knew what ailed Felicity. His name was Gus Pike.

Sara had been aware of Felicity's air of abstraction for some time. But it wasn't until her cousin dragged her out of the general store by the hand that she began to think seriously about the cause.

"I wanted to stay, Felicity!" she protested. "I like hearing Mr. Higgens talk."

"Don't be so selfish, Sara Stanley," retorted Felicity. "Think of someone else for a change. Think of me. Think of the agony I'm going through."

"Why, Felicity! I'm so sorry. I didn't know. Did you hurt yourself on the toboggan?"

"Oh for heaven's sake, Sara. Wake up. Can't you tell what the problem is?"

Sara inspected her cousin. All her limbs seemed intact. "No," she said finally. "You don't seem to be suffering from any serious injury. Perhaps it's internal. Perhaps you sprained something when you hit the snowbank?"

Felicity felt like screaming. "Of course it's internal, you little idiot. It's not a broken leg or a sprained ankle. It's something much, much worse."

"Hurry up and tell me, then. Quickly. What is it?"

Tears of self-pity flooded Felicity's eyes. "Gus Pike should have asked me to the Winter Festival by now."

It was Sara's turn to feel exasperated. Felicity was almost fifteen now, and she wished she would act her age. Even though she was only twelve, going on thirteen, quite often these days Sara felt as though she, not her cousin, were the elder of the two.

"Why, that's nothing," she replied sensibly, relieved that Felicity had not, after all, sustained some life-threatening injury. "All you have to do is remind him."

"Honestly, Sara, you talk as if you didn't know the first thing about boys. Boys never know what they want until you tell them yourself. That's why I need *you* to tell Gus what *he* wants. And as soon as possible. He should be back with Mr. Higgens's horse any second now."

"Why me? Why can't you tell him?"

"I couldn't possibly. You have to do it. If you don't, I'll never speak to you again, as long as I live."

As she spoke, Gus Pike rounded the corner, driving Mr. Higgens's buggy. Drawing up in front of the store, he waved cheerfully at the two girls. Felicity immediately stuck her nose in the air and walked away, leaving Sara stranded on the front steps.

"My, this poor old horse," said Gus, dismounting and running his hand soothingly down Bumbles's forehead and muzzle. "She's all rattled, so she is, just a mess of nerves. I feel real bad for frightening her like that, Sara." He did not appear to have noticed Felicity's departure.

Sara nodded. Out of the corner of her eye, she could see Felicity making furtive signals at her from behind the blacksmith's shed. "Go on. Ask him," her cousin was gesturing, using emphatic, pointing movements. "If not ..." She made a gesture across her mouth, as though sewing it shut.

Sara sighed. What if she refused to ask Gus about the Winter Festival? What if Felicity truly never did speak to her as long as she lived? Would that be so bad? There was, it seemed, a long history of people not speaking to each other in the King family. Numerous great-aunts and third cousins had gone silent to their graves, refusing to speak the word that might have resolved some long-held grievance. Did she want to add to that history? No, she decided, she did not. Besides, she loved Felicity. She would far rather be her friend and confidante than her enemy.

She turned to Gus, who was tying Bumbles's reins to the hitching post.

"I've just had the most marvelous idea, Gus," she said, as though suddenly inspired. "The Winter

Festival's coming up. And I suddenly thought—why don't you ask Felicity to the skating party?"

Gus lifted his head, turning his chin in the rather awkward manner he sometimes had. For a second his eyes looked straight over at Felicity, who was monitoring their conversation from the blacksmith's shed. Then he returned his attention to Sara. That one swift motion of his eyes startled her, for it was more revealing than words. A phrase her father had liked to quote floated into her head. "The mind has a thousand eyes and the heart but one ..." he used to say, referring to his love for her mother. Without appearing to notice, Gus had known exactly where Felicity was every second since he had driven up in the buggy. It was as though an inner eye were focused on her all the time, as though he were connected to her without being able to help it. This is what Felicity must be feeling too, thought Sara. The insight made her resolve to be more understanding of Felicity's moods in future.

Her question about the skating party still hovered in the air. It seemed to have thrown Gus into a quandary. He shuffled from foot to foot. "I dunno," he said hesitantly. "I ain't thought too much about it."

This was not the Gus Pike Sara knew speaking. The Gus Sara knew was straight as an elm, with level brown eyes that looked right at you and always told the truth. But today he stood beside her on the steps of Mr. Lawson's store, his head bent, his keen eyes averted from hers. Something was troubling him, she could tell. But she had no idea what it was. She waited a moment longer, hoping he would meet her gaze.

"Well, when you have thought it over, will you tell me?" she asked gently. Then she turned away to rejoin Felicity.

Gus stood where he was, his hand still on Bumbles's muzzle. He could feel Felicity's glance on him. He knew he had disappointed her. But he did not look at her. How could he? He would never be able to do what she wanted.

Chapter Four

Hetty was rinsing out the teapot when she spotted her neighbor, Wellington Campbell, through the kitchen window. He was striding around her back garden with a hammer in one hand, a toolbox in the other and a murderous expression on his face.

"What's Mr. Campbell doing out there in the snow?" asked Sara, joining her aunt at the window.

"I don't know. But whatever it is, I don't like it."

Hetty spooned tea into the fat brown pot, filled it with freshly boiled water and placed it on the table, covering it with a tea-cozy. It looked, thought Sara, as plump and comforting as a broody hen.

"Neighbors aren't supposed to trample through other people's gardens like that," continued Hetty, hovering about the table. She felt torn between her longing to find out what Mr. Campbell was up to and her urgent need of a cup of tea. "As soon as we've had our tea I shall go out and investigate. Yes, I do think that would be best. If I go out now, parched as I am, I shall only lose my temper. Now come and sit down, Sara."

A bouncy *rat-a-tat-tat* from the front door knocker made them both jump. Aunt Hetty almost dropped the teapot.

"Good heavens! Can't a body enjoy her tea in peace these days? You don't suppose it's that nasty Wellington Campbell, do you?"

"There's just one way to find out," said Sara, jumping up from the table.

But it was not Mr. Campbell, armed with toolbox and hammer, who stood at the front door. It was Wally Higgens, holding his sample case and preparing to launch into his sales patter. Seeing Sara, he took a step backwards. The deep breath he had inhaled came rushing back out in a wheeze of surprise.

"Why, looky here!" he exclaimed. "If it ain't one of my good Samaritans."

"Mr. Higgens! How nice to see you again!" said Sara.

Aunt Hetty looked from one to the other. "Might I ask how you two know each other?" she asked sternly.

Removing his hat, Wally bowed low before Aunt Hetty. "Higgens is the name. Skates the game, madam," he recited. "All the way from the Windy City and the Windy City Skate Company. Me and your—er—daughter, here —"

"Niece," interjected Sara.

"Me and your niece bumped into each other, in a manner of speaking, earlier today."

Dear God, thought Aunt Hetty to herself. A Yankee salesman. Would you just listen to his grammar? And at teatime, too! She nodded coldly at Mr. Higgens and his dreadful salesman's hat.

"I'm afraid I don't converse with traveling salesmen, Mr. Higgens. On principle. And I certainly have no need for —"

"Say no more, madam!" interrupted Wally. He could feel his salesman's blood rising to the challenge presented by this disapproving old hen. "Wouldn't life be dull if we only got what we need? Take diamonds, now. Who needs diamonds?"

Hetty made a dismissive gesture, implying that she neither knew nor cared.

"Quite right, madam. Nobody needs 'em. Yet who wants diamonds? Everyone. Without exception. Every little lady in the land." He edged his sample bag closer to the door. "Now, I want you to take a gander here at our brand new Windy City Special. Because skates like these will bring a sparkle just like diamonds to those big brown eyes, madam. No disrespect intended, of course," he added hastily, seeing Hetty stiffen with anger.

The insolence of the fellow! Hetty positively itched to slam the door in his face. Indeed, she would have done so long ago had Sara not been standing in the doorway, staring up at Mr. Higgens in fascination.

Sara had never heard anyone talk quite like Mr. Higgens. His particular combination of bad grammar, American slang and downright niceness appealed to her strongly. *Now looky here,* she repeated inwardly, *you just take a gander, little lady.* She hoped she would remember such expressions, so that she could try them out later on her friends.

Wally took full advantage of the momentary pause.

"Never been an offer like this here Windy City Special before, little ladies. Why, it's as good as two skates for the price of one. I'll also throw in, free of charge, a lifetime supply of laces. As well as ... " With a dramatic flourish he produced a small object from his pocket. "A portable skate-sharpener! Guaranteed for the life of the customer or the life of the skates, whichever kicks the bucket first. All free, gratis and for nothing!"

Kick the bucket, rejoiced Sara, silently, *free gratis and for nothing.*

But Aunt Hetty had had enough. Taking Sara by the elbow, she drew her back inside. "I'm sorry, Mr. Higgens," she said firmly, "but you are wasting your time." Her hand closed around the doorknob.

Not for nothing was Wally Higgens known as one of the best salesmen on the eastern seaboard. Long years in his profession had taught him to recognize imminent defeat and circumvent it. If that door slammed, all hope of a sale would be crushed. Wally did not enjoy failure. It made him nervous and irritable. Quick as a flash, he stuck his toe inside the door.

An expression of delight transformed his face. He inhaled deeply.

"Say is that fresh, homemade cake I smell?" It was not the first time Wally had tried this tack. He had never known it to fail. "Ten to one it's plum," he said, looking directly at Sara.

Sara did not disappoint him. "Why, yes, it is plum cake. Aunt Hetty made it. Why don't you join us for tea, Mr. Higgens?"

"Tea?" said Wally, his voice cracking with emotion in the most appealing way. "Tea? Why, I'd sell my soul for a nice hot drink. It's mighty hard on a feller selling door to door in this cold." He slipped his whole foot inside the door.

Aunt Hetty had no choice. She had to step back or risk being knocked over. She glared at Sara. But Sara had bent down and was helping Mr. Higgens drag his sample case inside the door. For a moment Hetty considered ordering Mr. Higgens out of her house, but to do so would mean breaking all the laws of hospitality. Her own niece had invited him for tea. This vulgar little man was their guest, and she would just have to put up with him. But only, she promised herself, for an hour.

Two hours later, Wally Higgens was still ensconced at Hetty's table, wolfing down plum cake and slurping cup after cup of tea. Yet, strange to say, Hetty made no move to force him to leave. Something about the rotund little salesman had begun to appeal to her. She found herself liking his unrestrained enthusiasm. But most of all, it was his isolation that wore down her defenses. How could you harden your heart against someone who came straight out and told you how lonely he was?

"Tea in the kitchen," Wally rhapsodized. "Home-made cake. Why, this sure beats hotels and restaurants. It's lonely being a traveling salesman, little ladies. A lonesome life on the lonesome road."

Hetty hesitated. She really should go out and check on Wellington Campbell. That man had been rampaging about her garden for hours now without so much as a by-your-leave. But she was reluctant to hurt Mr. Higgens by leaving. All the same, if she didn't go soon, it would be dark outside.

Getting up from the table, she fetched her boots. "I'm afraid you'll have to excuse me, Mr. Higgens," she said, with a nod and a smile. "But I must go see what my neighbor is plotting in my garden."

Wally Higgens rose quickly to his feet. "Say, don't apologize, ma'am. I should be going anyway. I don't want to overstay my welcome."

"No, please sit and finish your tea. I'll just change into my boots here, if you don't mind."

It was while she was lacing up her left boot, which she always did last, that Hetty became aware of Mr. Higgens's eyes. They seemed to burn a hole right through the leather, so intense and fixed was their gaze. She glanced around to see whether he might be looking at something else, beyond her toes. A fly on the wallpaper, perhaps, or a spot on the newly scrubbed floor. But no. It was her feet and her feet alone he was staring at, with naked admiration. Embarrassed, she stood up, covering both boots with her skirt.

Mr. Higgens caught her look of astonishment. "Forgive me," he urged. "Your feet. I can't help but stare. What ... what size are they?"

"Why, what a question, Mr. Higgens! I'm afraid I don't know. Size six, I think." Stooping, Hetty placed her shoes under the kitchen table.

Wally Higgens rose to his feet. The look on his face made both Hetty and Sara gasp. It was a look in which pain and delight seemed equally mixed. His voice sounded hoarse. "I'll bet they're quad A?"

Some of Hetty's original impatience with the man returned. "I really have no idea, Mr. Higgens." His question seemed to verge on impertinence. "I really can't see what business it is of yours, if you'll forgive my saying so." She offered him her hand. "Very pleasant to have met you," she said more gently. "Sara will see you out. Good day to you, Mr. Higgens." Without a backward glance she sailed out the door.

Wally Higgens sank down on the kitchen chair. Swooping up Hetty's shoes, he studied them for a second before dropping them, as though they'd burned his hands.

"Size six, quad A!" he breathed. "Size six. Quad A. I might have known!" He turned to Sara. "Your aunt ..." he whispered. "Not only is she a woman of breeding and brains. But she has the most perfect itsy-witsy tootsie-wootsies I have ever seen in the whole of my traveling life."

To Sara's amazement his eyes filled with tears. Why on earth should the size of Aunt Hetty's feet upset him so much?

Reaching out, Wally grabbed her hand. "I must call on her. I must, I must. Do I have even the remotest chance?"

Two tears spilled over and rolled down his plump cheeks.

Sara watched their course. She tried to interpret his agitation. "You mean, you like Aunt Hetty? You want to see her again? Is that what you mean?"

Wally nodded. He seemed unable to speak. Once again, his hands sought out Hetty's shoes. Lifting them from the floor, he placed them reverently on the kitchen table. His eyes closed as though in prayer. It seemed to Sara an age before he opened them again.

"It's like this, little lady," he said finally. "Your aunt is the woman of my dreams. If I don't win her, I shall die."

Chapter Five

On tiny perfect feet, Hetty tiptoed through the snow. The sky had cleared. The wintry sun lay low in the sky. Skeletal fruit trees rose up dark against the failing light.

Drat the man, thought Hetty, peering about. Now where has he got to?

Then she heard him, over by the apple trees Grandfather King had planted when his sons returned home from war. He seemed to be struggling with someone. Someone weaker than he, evidently, for with a grunt of victory Wellington Campbell lifted this person before her very eyes and hurled him into the snow.

"Great heavens!" thought Hetty, hurrying closer. "Has it come to this? An unseemly brawl in my own backyard?" Her heart beat faster, for now Mr. Campbell had picked up his hammer and was bending over his unfortunate victim. As he raised the heavy instrument, it gleamed dully in the setting sun. "Stop, Mr. Campbell! Stop at once!" she screamed, overcome with horror. "I'll not have you murdering people in my very own vegetable patch!"

Mr. Campbell straightened up, the hammer dangling from his hand.

"Ach, hold yer whist, woman," he snapped in his broad Scots brogue. "It's not your garden. It's mine. And I'll no have ye screaming blue murder in it!"

This outrageous claim on her property so stunned Hetty that for a moment she fell silent. Then she remembered her civic duty and bent quickly to assist Mr. Campbell's victim. But instead of a wounded man she saw nothing but a fence post. It was this that Mr. Campbell had wrestled with, wrenching it up from its rightful position in her ground. It was her fence post he had flung so triumphantly into the snow.

"Just what do you think you're doing?" Hetty

gasped. "You put my fence post back where it belongs this minute."

A smug look appeared on Wellington Campbell's long, bony face. "Your fence is on my property, Miss King."

"Rubbish!" snorted Hetty.

"I'll no argue with you, Miss King. All I'll say is that I have checked the relevant maps and it is my contention that a grievous error has been committed."

"Don't talk piffle, man. What sort of error?"

"An error of at least fifty feet!" pronounced Mr. Campbell. "Campbell property, according to my reading of the deeds, extends more than fifty feet beyond this old fence. That's why I'm tearing it down." He rocked back on his heels. "I canna have this old fence standing in the way of my new stables, now can I?"

"Stables? What stables?"

"The stables I'm planning to build on this here land of mine."

Outrage flooded Hetty. "May I remind you, Wellington Campbell, that this property has been in the King family for generations. Don't imagine for one second that you can snap your fingers and I'll just hand it over. You're not getting it. Not one speck of soil. Not one blade of grass. And that's final."

"Nothing's final until the lawyers have had their say, Miss King. So dinna lose your temper over it yet."

"I am NOT losing my temper!" yelled Hetty, purple with anger.

Wellington Campbell looked down at her from his lofty height. "My solicitor will be in touch with your solicitor, Miss King. In the meantime, let us try and keep our dignity, shall we? Good day to you." Dropping his hammer into his toolbox, he sauntered off, leaving Hetty's uprooted fence post lying at her feet.

She stood aghast. Visions of stallions snorting in her flowerbeds, scattering their droppings on her lawn, assailed her. Something must be done, and done at once. This very night she would assemble her family. Together they would decide what to do. "We'll settle your hash, Wellington Campbell," she declared grimly. She waited, as though expecting him to respond. But he had been swallowed up by the dusk. The fruit trees bent about her, still and dark. She was alone.

It was typical of Hetty that by the time Olivia and Janet arrived at Rose Cottage, she had already decided what she must do. Alec King was away in Charlottetown and Janet had brought the children, plus Daniel, the baby, with her. Hetty instructed Sara to take them upstairs. She did not want them interrupting her discussion with her sister and sister-in-law.

"He just can't do that, Hetty," exclaimed Olivia, her dark eyes growing round with indignation. "That land is our heritage. Our father left it to us. Just as Grandfather left it to him."

"Just wait till Alec gets back," snorted Janet. "He'll soon tweak that long Campbell nose."

"We will not wait for Alec to get back, Janet." Hetty spoke decisively. "We must strike while the iron is hot. I am the eldest in the family and it is my responsibility. I have reached a decision. First thing tomorrow I shall consult our solicitor in Carmody."

A knock on the door interrupted their conference. Hetty's eyebrows shot up. If this were Wellington Campbell, woe betide him! Stalking to the door, she threw it open, as though to say, "Advance, Wellington Campbell and meet your doom!"

Wally Higgens stood in the doorway, a bashful grin on his face, a box of chocolates in his hand. He looked, Hetty thought fleetingly, like a man out courting.

"Mr. Higgens!" she exclaimed. "At this hour of night? What can be the matter? Are you ill?"

Wally's smile spread from ear to ear. He smelled faintly of cologne. Extending the box to Hetty, he advanced farther into the room. "'Sweets to the sweet, hello,'" he simpered. "As ol' Willie used to say."

"If you're referring to William Shakespeare, Mr. Higgens, it was 'Sweets to the sweet, farewell.' Perhaps," she added hopefully, "you've come to say goodbye?"

Wally looked hurt. "Am I interrupting something?" he asked, eyeing Olivia and Janet, who stood staring at him in the most unladylike fashion from the kitchen.

"As a matter of fact, we were discussing some family business," said Hetty, edging him towards the door.

"In that case, I'd better mosey along." Wally looked crestfallen, but his tone remained cheerful. "You don't want no meddlesome city slicker nosin' in on family matters, now do you? But keep these anyways." He pushed the box of chocolates at Hetty. "Keep these. Think of me with every little bite."

Now it was Hetty's turn to blush. She glanced down at the artfully wrapped box. A discreet little gold seal in one corner announced that these chocolates had been confected in Brussels at the Maison Cornut. Hetty had never eaten Belgian chocolate before, but she knew its reputation. This unassuming little man with his dreadful grammar had bought these chocolates for her, Hetty King. How could she possibly ask him to leave?

"Why, Mr. Higgens, hello there! Felicity, Felix, Cecily! Come and see who's here!" Sara bounded downstairs, followed almost immediately by her cousins. The children flocked around Wally, drawing him farther into the warmth of the house.

Seeing the situation, Hetty submitted with as good a grace as she could muster. "Olivia, Janet." She did wish they would both stop gaping, slack-jawed, at the man. Surely they'd all seen a Yankee before. "I'd like you to meet Mr. Wally Higgens from Chicago."

Wally shook hands with the two women but refused to take off his coat. "No, no, no," he insisted, determined to prompt Hetty herself into extending the invitation this time. "Family business is family business. You don't want no outsiders. No, I'll just toodle on back to my cold little room at Mrs Biggins's and sit there all by my lonesome."

Hetty couldn't help it. She laughed. The man was so outrageous, what else could she do?

"Since you're here, you may as well come in and take a cup of something hot, Mr. Higgens," she said. "But you mustn't stay long. I've got to be up early in the morning."

Wally's face lit up. "You just talked me into it, little lady."

"Come along, Mr. Higgens. Felix will take your coat." Sara led Mr. Higgens into the parlor and pulled out a chair for him by the fire.

Olivia lingered by her sister. "Well, well, well. What a fine figure of a man, Hetty," she teased.

"Who? Wally Higgens? Why, he's homely as a stump fence!" sniffed Hetty. "Podgy too. Besides, his grammar's excruciating."

"Does any of that really matter?" Olivia smiled at her sister's indignant expression. "After all, he must have *some* redeeming features."

"Of course he does. He has wonderful taste in chocolates!" murmured Janet, joining them by the kitchen stove. "And if you don't hurry up and open them, Hetty King, I'll have to do it myself."

The rest of the evening passed like magic. Mr. Higgens kept everyone in hoots of laughter. He told jokes. He pulled a linen napkin from Cecily's ear. He found a marble in Felix's pocket that Felix had never seen before in his life. He read the tea leaves in Felicity's cup. He recited poetry for Sara. And though he favored everyone with his sunny smile, it was obvious that he had eyes only for Hetty.

Finally he sat back from the table with a sigh of delight. "That cake," he proclaimed. "That cake simply melts in your mouth. Who made it? An angel?"

Hetty smiled. Strange, she thought, she had not smiled so much in years. "Oh, that's nothing. Just an old recipe of my mother's."

Wally looked straight at her. "You should be married, you know. Why should Sara be the only one to enjoy your scrumptious cooking? Speaking of marriage ..." He looked around at the others. "What's the difference between a married man and a bachelor?"

"I don't know," answered Olivia. "You tell us."

"Your married man kisses the missus, see? And your bachelor misses the kisses!"

Amidst the general laughter, he rose reluctantly. "And now I'd better love you and leave you. I've a long road ahead of me tomorrow. Yours truly's driving over to visit the general store in Carmody first thing in the morning."

"Why, Hetty's going to Carmody tomorrow too!" exclaimed Olivia.

"Well now, isn't that a co-inky-dink!" Mr. Higgens flushed with pleasure. He looked down at Hetty. "What say we dipsy-doodle over there, you and me?"

Pointing his toes and crooking his elbow in the manner of a vaudeville dancer, he crooned, "You and me, me and you, add us up, we might make two." The soles of his feet brushed the floor rhythmically. He winked at the others. "One of my own inventions," he acknowledged modestly.

Co-inky-dink, dipsy-doodle. Suddenly Hetty wanted to put her head in her hands and moan. The very idea of spending hours alone in a buggy with a man who used such expressions made her brain ache. Yet only a minute ago she had been laughing at his jokes. She felt confused, and a little troubled.

"I couldn't ... couldn't possibly impose, Mr. Higgens," she protested feebly.

"Imposition! Why, I'd be honored, ma'am. I'll be at your gate, prompt as a crocus, at seven tomorrow morning. Goodnight now, and thanks muchly for the hospitality."

Before Hetty could open her mouth to refuse him, Wally had scampered off into the night.

Chapter Six

Wally was as good as his word. On the dot of seven the next morning his buggy drew up in front of Rose Cottage.

Through the lace curtains in the living room, Hetty watched him saunter up the walk, a dapper little man with a radiant smile. She had lain awake the night before, worrying about how she would cope with his sloppy grammar and insistent kindness. She had no desire to hurt his feelings, yet she could not abide improper speech. Now, seeing him, she felt these cares slip from her. The air was crisp and clear. The birds were singing. She had a lift into Carmody from a man who found her fascinating. What more could a woman ask? Straightening her wrap about her shoulders, she joined Wally Higgens on the front porch.

"Good morning, Hetty King." His smile lit up the porch like a beam from the lighthouse. "This Avonlea burg's sure got great air. And just listen to those birdies!"

Hetty's smile faltered. "Birdies, Mr. Higgens?"

Wally drew her arm through his as they walked down her path. "I think they're love birdies," he whispered.

Hetty withdrew her arm. She could not help it. She just could not stand by and hear the English language desecrated. "I hope you won't think me too particular, Mr. Higgens," she said carefully. "But those are birds, not birdies. Please call them by their proper name."

He chuckled. "I keep forgetting you're a schoolmarm." Helping her up into the buggy, he squeezed her hand. "I'll be your willing pupil, lamby-pie. Teach me whatever you like."

Lamby-pie! For a second, Hetty thought seriously of jumping out of the buggy and running off down the lane. Surely walking to Carmody in bare feet through the driving snow would be less painful than listening to words like *lamby-pie* and *birdy*. Get a grip on yourself, woman, she told herself sternly. Count to five and take a deep breath.

As long as Wally kept silent, the drive was pleasant enough. But talk came naturally to the sociable salesman. Having found the woman of his dreams, he wanted to envelop her in a warm cocoon of words.

"I don't know what it is about you, Hetty King," he blurted. "But when I'm around you, why, heck, I say whatever pops into my head. Things I wouldn't normally tell a soul."

Hetty was touched. "I can't say that people normally find me easy to talk to, Mr. Higgens. Quite the contrary."

"Well I do. Because I've seen your feet."

"I beg your pardon?"

Although Hetty's parents had never specifically said so, she had grown up with the impression that feet were a private matter. Not exactly in the same realm as undergarments, to which one never referred in public, but certainly to be touched on discreetly. For a near-stranger to refer so casually to her feet seemed somehow improper. Unconsciously, she pulled her long skirt more tightly about her ankles.

"No point in hiding 'em now. I've seen 'em, like I said. And let me tell you, they're perfect."

"Now look here, Mr. Higgens. Couldn't we talk of something else?"

"Size six. Quad A," he rhapsodized, unheeding. "I've said it before and I'll say it again. They're perfect feet—polite, genteel, but determined, too. They're no-nonsense feet. The tootsies of a no-nonsense kinda gal."

Tootsies. Kinda gal. Hetty winced. This time, she counted to ten.

"I will admit the no-nonsense part is true, Mr. Higgens," she conceded at last.

"Please don't call me Mr. Higgens. My name is Wally. Wally, Wally, Wally."

Hetty attempted a smile. "Wally, then. If you insist."

Wally sat up straighter in his seat. He twitched Bumbles's reins. "It makes me right proud to hear you say my name, Hetty." Turning, he inspected her profile. "Aintcha dyin' to know what *my* tootsies say about *me*?" he asked.

Hetty did not dare risk an honest answer to this question. But Wally seemed not to notice. He looked down at his shoes.

"They say that I've plied my wares from Lake Superior to Charleston and that they're sick and tired of my being alone." He looked over at her. "Don't you ever get lonesome, sugar dumpling?"

Sugar dumpling! Dear God in heaven tonight, what would the man say next? Hetty clutched her basket, feeling she had reached her limit. Should she jump off the buggy this very minute? Drawing a deep breath, she closed her eyes, preparing to leap.

When she opened them again, she saw that the buggy was passing through Avonlea. There on the sidewalk stood Clara Potts chatting with Elvira Lawson. Were she to jump now, they would surely see her. She could just imagine the fever of gossip and speculation to which such a move would give rise. With a shudder, she shrank back against the seat, drawing her wrap about her face. Perhaps if she kept very still they might not notice her. They might not nudge each other and point in amazement at Hetty King, the Avonlea schoolmistress, sitting in intimate proximity to a Yankee salesman in a loud check suit. Her eyelids fluttered closed. If she didn't look at them, perhaps they wouldn't see her. She prayed this might be so. She prayed, too, that Mr. Higgens would keep quiet, that he would not draw attention to them both.

After a moment she opened her eyes and found Mr. Higgens staring at her, obviously waiting for something. An answer, perhaps? But what was the question? All she had heard was *sugar dumpling* .

"I said, don't you ever get lonesome?" he repeated now, wondering why Hetty's face seemed suddenly obscured by her wrap.

"Me? I mean, I? Why no, of course not. I'm much too busy raising Sara and teaching school to grow lonesome, as you call it."

"But what about these long winter nights? Don't you ever long for someone to talk to?"

It was true. Sometimes she did long for someone to confide in, especially when Sara was tucked up in bed and she herself sat sleepless downstairs by the fire, worrying about one problem or another.

"Oh no," she lied. "Hardly ever. I tend to make a nice hot cup of tea and read a good book. The Bible, for instance."

"The Bible!" exclaimed Wally. She did wish he would keep his voice down. "Say, ain't that a co-inky-dink! That's my favorite book. Next to the skate catalogue, of course." Opening his mouth in what looked like a grimace, he broke into loud, tuneless song. *"Amaaay-ziiiing Gray-ce ..."*

"Shhh! Oh, please. Shhh!" pleaded Hetty.

But it was too late. All along the main street, the people of Avonlea stopped whatever they were doing and turned to stare. They gaped at Hetty King, sitting in the buggy of a strange man. They gaped at the stranger, who was emitting raucous, discordant noises at the top of his voice. The polite amongst them moved out of earshot as quickly as possible, but some rude folks even stuck their fingers in their ears as the buggy passed by. Others hurriedly closed their doors and windows.

Hetty thought she would die of mortification. She moved as far away from Wally as she could without falling off the seat. How else could she make it clear that, although she might be travelling in the same buggy with the man, he had nothing to do with her, Hetty King, champion of the King's English, mistress of Avonlea Public School and conductor of the Avonlea Public School choir?

Only when they had passed through Avonlea and were on the Carmody road did she relax slightly. Never, ever again, she thought with a shudder, will I experience such profound humiliation.

But she was wrong.

Hetty's second public humiliation came shortly after her visit to her solicitor in Carmody. She had emerged from his office flushed with triumph, clutching the property deed and maps in her gloved hand.

"Excellent news!" she called to Wally, who stood waiting outside by the buggy. "It appears that Mr. Campbell hasn't a leg to stand on." Yet it was not Mr. Campbell but Hetty who lost her balance, as she navigated her way around a snowdrift. Had Wally not reached out and caught her, she would have gone sprawling on her face in the slush.

What happened next was almost worse than a face full of slush, for just as Wally caught her in his arms, pressing her firmly against his rescuing chest, who should sail by but Eulalie Bugle.

"Poopsie Doodles!" exclaimed Wally, his voice loud with concern. "Tell me you ain't hurt?"

Poopsie Doodles?

"Don't shout so!" moaned Hetty, knowing full well that for lungs like Wally's, a whisper was as good as a roar. Of course Eulalie must have heard what he said. Of course she must have seen Wally's arms wrapped around Hetty. Of course the news would soon be spread all over Avonlea.

And yet, in the very moment of her second humiliation, Hetty could not help noticing that something was amiss with Eulalie. For instead of pausing to point fingers or ask questions, Mrs. Bugle simply walked right on by, her face averted. For some reason, she carried her bulging shopping basket tucked under her arm, as though to shield it from passers-by.

For as long as she could remember, Hetty had had little time for Eulalie Bugle. But since Olivia's wedding, she'd found it hard even to be civil to the woman. After all, as Hetty would ask anyone who cared to listen, how in the name of Providence could she be expected to exchange pleasantries with someone who would stoop low enough to snatch the wedding dress off Olivia's back? This was not exactly what Mrs. Bugle had done, but she had made the mistake of planning her daughter Cornelia's wedding on the same day as Olivia's. And as if this were not bad enough, she had then ordered exactly the same wedding dress from the catalogue. To top it all, her oversized daughter had mistakenly been sent Olivia's dress, while Olivia, slim as a trout, as Hetty put it, had received Cornelia's. Only Hetty's swift action had averted disaster on the wedding day. Even now, long after the event, Hetty found it hard to forgive Eulalie.

Mrs. Bugle never expressed how she felt about Hetty, but Hetty suspected that Eulalie would jump at the chance to slander her. Now she had it. Now she could run back to Avonlea and report that she had seen Hetty King cavorting in the arms of Wally Higgens. Why, then, did Eulalie slip past them, shoulders hunched, hugging the wall, like a thief in the night? It was, thought Hetty, as though Eulalie herself had some shameful secret, which she did not wish to share with anyone.

She was still puzzling over this abnormal behavior

on Mrs. Bugle's part when Wally dropped her off at her own front door.

"Thank you so much for the ride," she said insincerely. "I had a wonderful time. I do hope I can return the favor some day."

"Why wait for some day?" answered Wally. He must have been plotting this response all the way home, because the next question slipped right out, smooth as a seal. "Why don't you come to that skating party with me? That's all the favor I ask."

"The Winter Festival? Oh no ... I don't think so. I ... um ..." Hetty cast about for some excuse.

Wally gazed at her pleadingly. "Say yes, please, honey-bunny. One teensy tiny 'yes.'"

"Really, Mr. Higgens. You go too far!" Was Hetty mistaken or had she caught a glimpse of Sara and Olivia peeking out the front door? She did hope they hadn't heard *honey-bunny*.

"Jiminy, I'd have thought an important gal like yourself would be goin' anyways. Not waitin' about for some man to ask her."

"Well, yes, of course, I was thinking of going, only ..."

"Yippee and Hallelujah! So now you're goin' with me, steada goin on your lonesome. I'll come by to collect you on the day. See ya in my dreams, poopsie."

With a wave of his hand, Wally turned Bumbles and headed back to Mrs. Biggins's boarding house, leaving Hetty standing by her gate, wanting to scream with frustration.

Chapter Seven

Olivia and Sara were waiting for Hetty in the hall. As soon as she stepped in the door, they broke into Mendelssohn's "Wedding March."

"Here comes the bride," they shouted, dancing around Hetty. "Short, fat and wide ..."

"Stop that! Both of you!" shrilled Hetty. "Olivia, you should know better at your age. And you a married woman, into the bargain."

"I'll see you in my dreams, poopsie ..." giggled Olivia, chucking her elder sister under the chin. "Jiminy, but you're a honey-bunny!"

"How could you eavesdrop like that?" Hetty hung her wrap in the closet and turned to take off her boots. She felt worn out and dispirited, too tired even to share the good news about the property line with Olivia. "Go ahead and have tea without me," she said now, longing for a little peace and quiet.

Something in her tone alerted Sara. "Don't you like Wally, Aunt Hetty? He certainly admires you!"

"Like? How can I like anyone who constantly assaults the King's English? It's plain criminal, so it is. What that man does to words should be outlawed! *Co-inky-dink. Dipsy doodle. Honey-bunny. Poopsie-woopsie. Tootsie-wootsie. Lamby-pie!* Baby talk. That's what it is!"

As she pronounced the words, doing a passable imitation of Wally, Hetty couldn't help laughing, and neither could Sara and Olivia. They were such outrageously silly words.

"It's not baby talk, Hetty. It's love talk," Olivia observed.

"It's ridiculous, whatever you call it. Jasper doesn't talk to you like that, surely?"

The idea of her absentminded husband addressing her in such a way made Olivia laugh even harder. "He'd die first. But all the same, Hetty." Olivia grew serious."It seems a shame to throw away a perfectly nice man just because of his grammar."

"Throw away? The man's not mine to throw away. I've only just met him."

Olivia looked over at her niece. "Go make the tea, Sara. Don't include me, though. I won't be staying. I promised Jasper I'd be home in time for tea with him."

Once Sara had left the room, Olivia turned to her sister.

"Really, Hetty," she said, as she pinned on her hat. "For a well-educated woman, you can sometimes be extremely slow."

"Slow?"

"Do you want to be left all alone in your old age?"

"What in the name of heaven does my age have to do with Wally Higgens?"

"He admires and likes you, anyone can see that. He's anxious to settle down."

"Nobody's stopping him."

"With you. He'd like to settle down with you."

"Don't talk nonsense, Olivia. I'm much older than he is."

"I don't see what that matters, if you like each other."

"I never said I like him."

Olivia took her sister's arm. "Forgive my saying this, Hetty, but you're getting on in life. Who's going to look after you? Who's going to bring you hot milk in the middle of the night when you're not feeling well? Sara won't live here forever, you know. One of these days she'll be off to some finishing school or other in Switzerland. And where will you be then?"

"Right here where I belong," retorted Hetty, yanking her arm out of Olivia's grasp.

"Exactly," responded Olivia, stung by Hetty's abrupt rejection. "You'll be right here. All alone."

The words hung in the air, gloomy, slightly menacing. But Olivia made no move to retract them. She finished putting on her coat, pecked her sister on the cheek, hugged Sara and left.

Hetty went to her room early that evening. She needed to collect her thoughts, to reflect in silence on the day's events. Olivia's words had disturbed her. They implied that living on one's own was something to be feared. Hetty was not sure this was true, but she had not yet disproved it. She had not yet lived on her own for any length of time. Since Alec's marriage to Janet many years ago, Hetty and Olivia had shared Rose Cottage. Then their niece, the motherless Sara

Stanley, had arrived in Avonlea. Hetty and Olivia had taken the child to live with them, since the King farmhouse was already bursting at the seams with children and animals. Later, Olivia had met and married Jasper Dale, but Sara's presence at Rose Cottage had helped dim the loneliness Hetty felt after her sister's departure. Now Sara was growing up. One of these days she, too, would leave. Olivia was certainly right about that. Hetty would be all alone. How would she react? Would she enjoy her aloneness? Or would she fall to pieces?

Hetty sighed and sat down at her dressing table. Olivia seemed to be implying that any man was better than none. Could that be true? She looked around her bedroom, at the familiar furniture, the drawings and photographs carefully collected over the years, each one with a story behind it. She looked at the curtains, which she had stitched herself, when she and Olivia had first moved from the King farmhouse to Rose Cottage. How excited they had been, setting up house together, on their own! How they had schemed and dreamed and laughed! She smiled at the memory.

And her books. Reaching out, she ran her hand lovingly over the rows of books standing on the shelves near her bed. She had read and reread each one. These books had been her friends and mentors. They had taught her, guided her, given her comfort in times of unhappiness. They were as much a part of her as her arms and legs. Legs. Feet. Tootsie-wootsies. With a bump, her thoughts returned to Wally Higgens.

"Lamby-pie," she muttered, squinting at her reflection in the dressing-table mirror. "Mutton-pie, more likely." She ran a finger over the wrinkles lining her eyes. Olivia was right. She was growing older by the minute. But did that mean she had to rush into matrimony with the first man to offer?

Not that Wally Higgens was the first. There had been Romney Penhallow, for one. Not to speak of that fraud, Ambrose Dinsdale. He of the beguiling voice and the many wives.

"He's almost certain to be the last, though," she said aloud. Picking a rose from a vase on her dressing table, she sniffed it distractedly. Of course, she shouldn't forget that Wally hadn't exactly besought her hand in matrimony. Not yet. The thought that he might actually come right out and ask her to marry him, in his horrible, fractured English, filled her with distaste. She tried not to think of the many slang phrases he might use, but they came flooding into her mind, unbidden. She held the rose against her throat, also badly wrinkled, she noted.

"Hey, poopsie, wanna get hitched, wanna tie the knot, wanna get spliced?" she asked her reflection. The look on her own face made her laugh. She had to admit that admiration, even from Wally Higgens, was good for the spirit. Remembering his infectious enthusiasm, she looked at herself sternly. "You think you're so superior," she scolded. "What gives you the right to sneer at Wally Higgens? He's a decent man. I'll bet he makes a decent living. You should count yourself lucky."

Her image looked duly abashed. "There are lots of prettier women in this world, all of them probably dying to marry Wally Higgens," she continued, pinning the rose in her hair to check the effect. "So stop sticking your nose in the air, Lady Muck."

Outside her aunt's door, Sara paused in surprise, her hand raised to knock. She could hear voices. Surely Aunt Hetty could not be entertaining someone in her bedroom? She had always told Sara that friends were to be entertained in the parlor, not the bedroom. Whenever she found any of Sara's friends in her room she had always shooed them downstairs, no matter how inconvenient it was for them. Once Felicity had been in the middle of squeezing herself into one of Sara's party dresses and Aunt Hetty had pushed her downstairs with the dress half on and half off!

Sara looked down at the arithmetic exercise in her hand. She had been hoping Aunt Hetty would help her with the hard problems. She was anxious to finish up, so she could go to bed. Pressing her ear against the door, she listened. Whoever was in there seemed unable to get a word in edgeways. Aunt Hetty was doing all the talking. She sounded like she was scolding the person's ear off. Perhaps her visitor needed rescuing. Without waiting for a reply, Sara knocked and walked in.

Aunt Hetty sat at her dressing table, a rose in her hair, her mouth open. There was no one else in the room. Seeing Sara, she colored with embarrassment and began pulling the flower from her graying head.

"No, don't take it out," Sara said. "It looks pretty."

"Piffle!" Hetty 's voice was brisk to hide her discomfort. "I'm a plain woman and no rose is going to alter that."

"How can you say that? Anyone with an imagination can see that you have a fascinating face. A face full of stories. I'm sure Mr. Higgens doesn't think you're plain."

"Higgens, Higgens, Higgens!" exploded Hetty, flinging the rose into the waste basket. "I wish the women in this family would stop badgering me about Wally Higgens!"

"But we're excited for you, Aunt Hetty."

"For heaven's sake, stop talking as though I'm about to get spl—, I mean, married. I am going to the Winter Festival, child, that's all."

A smile touched the corners of Aunt Hetty's thin lips. "I, Hetty King, who cannot skate for toffee, am going to the skating party with a skate salesman who calls me poopsie-woopsie."

Chapter Eight

Rupert Gillis raced after Felicity. He had hoped to catch her on her own, but she had left school with her cousin Sara and would probably walk all the way home with her. He couldn't afford to wait another day. He had to ask her now.

As he caught up with the two girls, he contrived to part them, steering Felicity slightly ahead of Sara with his arm. He hoped that Sara would have the decency to hang back a bit, granting him some time alone with Felicity.

"Say, Felicity," he began, feeling his courage suddenly ebb as she looked at him with those lovely eyes of hers, which reminded him of the lavender growing in his mother's garden. He pulled his cap from his head. "How 'bout you and me ... I mean ... would you come with me to the skating party? Together? You and me? The two of us?" He could feel the sweat breaking out under his collar.

Felicity glanced at him, then glanced back at Sara. She walked on hastily as though she, too, wished to put some distance between herself and her cousin.

In the distance, Rupert could see Felix running behind Sara, trying to catch up with her. He hoped Sara would stop him when he reached her and not let him come barging in on his conversation with Felicity. Not that you could call it a conversation. Felicity had not yet said a word, although she had flushed at the first mention of the skating party.

Rupert felt hope leap in his heart. She had not said no. But then, she had not said yes, either. Glancing at her more closely, he saw that she was fighting back tears. He hoped he had not offended her. He had tried to be polite and respectful, in the way a book he had read recently had instructed. It belonged to his sister Ruby and was called *The Laws of Etiquette*. He had struggled through chapter after chapter on "The Importance of

Early Moral Instruction," "Pen and Pencil Flourishing" and "Bad Habits of Horses," without finding anything that seemed of use. Finally he had come across a page headed "What to Avoid in Social Conversation." This he had committed to memory. He repeated some of it to himself now, to bolster his courage. "Do not manifest impatience. Do not appear to notice inaccuracies of speech in others. Do not make a parade of your emotions. Do not yield to bashfulness." Well, he certainly hadn't yielded to bashfulness. He had spoken up like a man. He walked on through the snow with Felicity, waiting for her to gain control of her tears and answer his question. *Do not manifest impatience.*

At last she spoke. "Thank you for asking, Rupert," she said. "But I can't go with you. I am already spoken for."

He stared at her. *Do not appear to notice inaccuracies of speech in others.*

Rupert might sometimes be late handing in his school essays, but he had done his homework where Felicity was concerned. He had made inquiries of every eligible male in Avonlea, and not one had been able to claim he had invited Felicity to the skating party. Not even Gus Pike, who had been first on Rupert's list. Gus had merely shaken his head when Rupert asked him. But there had been a dangerous look in his eyes, which had made Rupert take one step back.

Now he felt confused. Either he had missed one of Avonlea's most eligible names from his list. Or Felicity was lying. And why had those tears come into her eyes? What did it all mean? She was looking at him now, with sympathy, it seemed. He felt like hurling himself at her feet and pleading with her to reconsider.

Do not make a parade of your emotions. Rupert Gillis bowed politely. He put his cap back on his head. "Never mind, Felicity," he said bravely. "I'll see you in school tomorrow." He walked away, struggling with his own tears.

Behind them, Sara had heard every word. Now she and Felix caught up with Felicity.

"That was a big fat lie, Felicity King," Sara scolded her.

"Yeah," added Felix. "That was a whopper if ever I heard one."

Felicity walked on, looking miserable. "It was only half a lie, and I only did it to spare Rupert's feelings. I can't go to the skating party with him. What would Gus think? I *am* spoken for, truly I am. I know Gus will ask me. It's just he hasn't asked me yet."

Felix shook his head. "He ain't gonna ask you. He said as much to me himself."

"It's none of your business. Besides, what do you know about it?"

"I asked him, that day you sent me over to the lighthouse with sandwiches. I knew you wanted me to ask. So don't pretend you didn't."

Felicity had turned white. "You asked him? And he said no?"

"That's what he said. Said he had too many other

things to do. Hey, where are you going, Felicity? Felicity! Come back!"

But Felicity had taken to her heels. She ran wildly, as though pursued by someone or something. She ran blindly too, as though something were in her eyes, obscuring her vision.

Sara reached out and patted Felix on the shoulder. "Never mind," she said. "I'll walk home with you."

As soon as Sara had accompanied Felix back to the King farm, she turned her steps in the direction of the lighthouse, where Gus had lived on his own since the departure of the lighthouse keeper, the mysterious Ezekiel Crane.

Gus was sitting on an overturned barrel, mending a net. He didn't seem in the least surprised to see her.

"Now look," she said, plunging right in, "the skating party's going to be fun. Why don't you ask Felicity and get it over with? Don't you want to ask her?"

"It ain't that ..." Gus's eyes were fixed on the net.

"What is it, then?"

This time he looked at her directly. "You might as well know now as later, I guess," he said hesitantly. "I ain't got no skates."

"Is that all?"

Relief made Sara smile. She had imagined all sorts of terrible reasons why Gus should torture himself and Felicity, but nothing as simple as a lack of skates. "Why on earth didn't you say so straight out?"

"Easy for you to talk." He gazed out across the bay. "You were born with a silver spoon in your mouth, Sara. You've never had to work for every single solitary thing you need in life."

Sara had never heard him speak like this before, in a tone more tired than bitter. It was true that she had been born into a moneyed background, into a family that seemed to acquire or lose wealth as effortlessly as some people find and lose mittens. But her life had not been easy either. Her mother had died when Sara was very young. Her father had never quite recovered from this loss, and Sara had endured a lonely, isolated childhood with only her elderly Nanny Louisa for company. Then had come her father's financial problems and, shortly afterwards, his death in an accident.

It was her relatives in Avonlea who had saved Sara. Their love and easygoing acceptance had drawn her back from the brink of desolation. They had fed her, housed her, scolded and comforted her. They had provided her with the family she needed. No longer did she feel like a lonely outsider, wandering on the brink of life. She felt she belonged.

Despite this wonderful new sense of family and the knowledge that she had inherited a large fortune, Sara had not forgotten the insecurities of her earlier years. Anyone who has once felt like an outsider cannot help but recognize the same feeling in others. Gus was an outsider. He too had lost his mother at an early age. He had lost his father as well.

Here the similarities ended, for Gus's father had been a violent, uncaring man, who had abandoned his wife and child. After his mother's death, Gus had been placed in an orphanage. Some of his bitterest memories stemmed from this period. He could still hear the callous laughter of the other children when, a small, bewildered boy, he had wept into his soup the day of his arrival, unable to hide his grief at his mother's death. He remembered the cold, dreary dormitories, the coarse sheets, which often felt wet from damp, the stone floors under his bare feet. He remembered the constant ache of hunger, the frequent punishments, the little cruelties that children who have been treated badly learn to inflict on each other. Above all, he remembered the many nights he spent praying for his father to return and rescue him. But never once did he hear from Abraham Pike. Never a visit, never even a letter.

Occasionally, though, a package would be handed in to the orphanage for Gus Pike. Clumsily wrapped, it might contain a pair of boots, sized just right, or a warm scarf, not always new. Once, miraculously, a fishing rod. No note was ever attached. At first, Gus hoped against hope that these gifts came from his father. But gradually he began to suspect another source, for the nature of the gifts indicated a perceptiveness his father lacked. It dawned on Gus that someone in the outside world was watching over him. Someone was taking note of how he was growing, what his needs were. And although he was disappointed that this anonymous benefactor was not his father, the knowledge that someone cared about him restored his hope and, with it, his desire to live.

Eventually, after he had left the orphanage and come to live and work in Avonlea, Gus learnt that his anonymous savior was none other than Ezekiel Crane, the lighthouse keeper.

Once, many years ago, Ezekiel had been one of Eliza MacLeod's two suitors. Abraham Pike had been the other, a laughing, shiftless charmer. Eliza had chosen Abraham and almost instantly regretted it. In the end, when she lay dying, it was Ezekiel who had cared for her, Ezekiel who had promised to keep an eye on her small son. In his own rough way, he had been true to his word. Gus would always be grateful to him for that. In his mind he acknowledged that this unkempt, solitary stranger had been more of a father to him than his own.

Looking back on it all now, he felt that in many ways he had been one of the luckier children in that orphanage. After all, thanks to the kindness of Ezekiel, he had emerged from his experiences there with some sense of his own worth. Except for the odd bout of depression, his cheerful disposition remained intact. He stirred now, trying to shake off the feeling of loss that sometimes sprang out at him from his memories.

"Most times it don't seem so bad. I'm young and strong. Willing, too. I can work for what I need. Only sometimes ..."

His dark eyes clouded, and Sara knew he was

❧❧❧

"Put 'em up, smelly ol' Welly!" Mr. Higgins taunted.
"Face me if you dare! Galoshes! Rubbers!
Wellington boots! Ha! What kind of a name is that
for a fella?"

❦❦❦

"Please keep the skates, Hetty King,"
Wally Higgins said, flicking the reins at Bumbles.
"I wouldn't want anyone else in the world
to wear them."

❦❦❦

"Oh cripes! Now we've done it!" gasped Felix.
"He's dead!"
"It's all my fault!" wailed Sara.

❦❦❦

"Just what do you think you're doing?" Hetty gasped.
"You put my fence post back where it belongs
this minute." A smug look appeared on
Wellington Campbell's long, bony face.
"Your fence is on my property, Miss King."

thinking of Felicity and the home of plenty and comfort she came from. Placed beside what she had, his little accomplishments seemed dwarfed.

"Sometimes I think I got everything all planned out, like, and then something like this here skatin' party comes along. An' I can't afford to buy no skates. An' I just get tired of never being able to afford nothin'. I hate havin' to admit it all the time. Havin' to say I can't afford this. I can't spend the money on that. I got my pride, Sara."

Sara nodded in silent understanding. After a while she asked, "If you had skates, would you ask Felicity to the skating party?"

"Sure I would. There'd be nothin' stoppin' me then. Leastways not unless someone else asks her first." His face darkened. "That young Rupert Gillis, he's hopin' she'll go with him. He's after her, I can tell."

"He already asked her. She turned him down."

"She did? She turned Rupert Gillis down? Why'd she do that?"

"Why, Gus Pike, can't you even see the nose in front of your face? She's waiting for you to ask her. "

His eyes lit up. "That Felicity King," he murmured. "Ain't she just a wonder?"

Sara hesitated. An idea had come to her, but she was nervous about broaching it, knowing how proud he was.

"Look, Gus, Uncle Alec has at least two pairs of old skates he never uses. I think one belonged to his younger brother. If I brought them over, would you try them on?"

It was growing dark. The wind had risen. Overhead seagulls circled, filling the air with their cries. Then, suddenly, they wheeled off into the Gulf. In the quiet that followed their flight, the pounding of the waves on the rocks below seemed thunderous.

Gus looked at Sara for a second before replying. Ever since coming to Avonlea he had been grateful for the kindness of the King family, but Sara in particular had been a friend to him. She never sat in judgment. She listened. She always tried to help.

Standing up, he shook out the finished net before folding it. "That's mighty kind of you, Sara. I'd be real grateful."

"I'll bring them over after supper tomorrow."

He grinned at her suddenly. "You'll have to show me how to lace 'em up. I ain't never had skates before."

"Never?"

"Not in my whole life."

"What about lessons, then? Maybe I should give you some."

"Just show me how to lace 'em. I'll figure the rest out for myself. It can't be too hard, can it? I seen Felix do it."

"I don't mind giving you lessons, honestly."

"Naw. You done enough for me, Sara. I appreciate it, truly I do. I'll learn to skate on my own, don't you worry. After all, if you can walk, you can skate. Ain't that so?"

He smiled down at her, his confidence restored.

She hated to contradict him, to risk seeing that brooding look return. "I guess it's like anything else," she replied carefully. "It's easy once you know how. I'd love to give you a lesson or two, though."

Gus raised his head to the darkening sky. He could smell more snow on the way.

"Never you mind about lessons. You go on home now," he said solicitously. "It's getting late. I'll talk to Felicity in the morning."

Chapter Nine

The morning after her visit to Carmody, Hetty rose early and was out in the garden just as the birds were stirring. Picking up the fence posts dislodged by Wellington Campbell, she hammered each one back into its rightful place. She hummed as she worked, the encouraging words of her solicitor dancing in her mind.

"Not a leg to stand on, tra-la-la," she warbled, pounding on the post. "We'll lead that man a merry dance through the courts, ho ho ho!"

Now Wellington Campbell was an elderly man, but he was not deaf. Alerted by Hetty's thumpings and trillings, he left his bed, dressed himself and hurried outside. Striding up to his neighbor, he seized the post she was holding and tried to wrest it from her, forgetting, it must be said, all precepts of gentlemanly conduct.

But Hetty could override the rules of ladylike behavior too, when the occasion warranted. Refusing to let go, she yanked the fence post right back.

"Now just what do you think you're doing, Hetty King?" demanded Wellington Campbell. "And so early in the morning, too?"

"I'm hammering the King fence back onto King property. That's what I'm doing, Wellington Campbell. And there's nothing you can do about it. Look!" Pulling her precious documents from the pocket of her coat, she waved them under Mr. Campbell's nose.

"Why, this is nothing but legal hocus-pocus!" he snorted, unrolling the papers and scanning them quickly.

"Hocus-pocus or no, it was you who threatened to involve solicitors. If you wish to proceed further, you will have to wade through a lot more hocus-pocus from my lawyers!"

Mr. Campbell looked at her sharply. Had she discovered some legal loophole through which she now intended to creep? Perhaps he should read these documents more carefully. Resting his hand on the fence post, he began at the beginning.

Hetty concentrated on ensuring that the ground around the fence post was firmly packed. Then, raising her hammer, she brought it down on the post with as much strength as she could muster.

"Owwwwwwww!!!!"

Mr. Campbell leapt up, scattering the papers to the four winds. Hetty had not been looking at the fence post. Without meaning to, she had hammered Mr. Campbell's thumb.

"Dear God," she gasped, clapping her fingers against her mouth. "Oh how dreadful. I'm terribly, terribly sorry!" She reached out to see how bad the wound was.

Mr. Campbell snatched his hand away. "Don't you touch me!" he roared, his face mottled with fury. "You haven't heard the last of this, Hetty King! Not by a long shot!"

Turning, he lumbered back to his house, like a wounded bear clutching its paw.

Hetty's knees felt weak. How could she have been so clumsy? What if she had permanently injured Wellington Campbell? She stumbled about the garden, gathering up the legal papers. She no longer felt like singing. She rolled the papers together carefully and placed them on a shelf in the kitchen. Then she returned to the fence posts, but all joy had gone out of her work. A sense of dread hung over her. The idea of hurting another human being appalled her. Somehow it seemed even worse to hurt someone with whom she was on bad terms. Yet she had not done it deliberately.

She was working in another part of the garden, pulling up the stakes and the rope Wellington Campbell had used to mark his version of the property line, when Wally Higgens drove up in his buggy.

He parked in front of the house, entered the garden

and crept up behind her so quietly that she was unaware of his presence.

"BOO!" a male voice yelled, making her jump skywards.

Her heart pounding, she turned to find Wally grinning at her. He was the last person she felt like seeing.

"Gracious Providence!" she gasped. "You scared me half to death."

Dimples danced in Wally's round cheeks. He held both hands behind his back. "I've brought a little present for my sweetcakes!"

Sweetcakes? God give me strength, she thought. She turned away from him wearily, heading back to her fence. "Not now, Wally, she said. "I'm busy this morning."

But Wally would not be put off so lightly. He danced in front of her, holding out a pair of tiny, delicate skates. "Roses are red," he intoned. "Candy is sweet. I love my poopsie for the size of her feet." He beamed proudly. "Made that up myself this morning, 'specially for you, poopsie."

Hetty took a deep breath. She turned to face him, pronouncing each syllable carefully and distinctly, as though to a person slow in understanding.

"I know you mean well, Wally. But I cannot accept any more gifts. Besides, I can't even skate. No. Thank. You."

As Hetty said later to Sara, she might as well have saved her breath to cool her porridge. Wally paid absolutely no attention.

"You have to take them. You must wear them,

please. At the skating party. These skates are vitally important, poopsie. If only you knew how much they mean to me!"

Over Wally's shoulder, Hetty saw Wellington Campbell hobble out his front door and turn in the direction of his stable, holding his wounded arm straight out in front of him, as though to ward off other possible attackers wielding hammers. He was dressed in his Sunday-go-to-meeting clothes.

Hetty sat down abruptly on a stump, filled with foreboding. Mr. Campbell was heading into Carmody. Of that she felt sure. There was a surgeon in Carmody. Could he be going to have his thumb amputated? Perhaps his whole hand? Or even his arm? She felt sick with worry.

Wally interpreted her sitting down as a sign of acquiescence. He knelt in front of her, dangling the skates.

"Try 'em on, honey-bunny," he pleaded. "Just try 'em on. I'm dying to see if they fit."

Hetty was too distressed to protest. Wearily she began to remove her boots, feeling like an ancient Cinderella.

If only Hetty had been paying attention, she might have avoided the calamity that later erupted. But her mind was filled with her battle with Wellington Campbell. There was no room in it to consider Wally, or to wonder what plot he was hatching in his own mind.

A perceptive observer would have seen that Wally

was bubbling over with excitement. He had devised his own plan of action in his courtship of Hetty King and he was determined to seek her advice in the matter, whether she was aware of what he was doing or not. Unfortunately for her, Hetty was not a perceptive observer.

"Tell me something, sugar dumpling." Wally polished the gleaming skates absentmindedly with his cuff as he waited for Hetty to finish unlacing her boots.

"What is it, Wally?"

"What if there was something that was real important to you —"

"You mean, really important?"

"Yeah, real significant. Something that you wanted more than anything in the world. What would you do, Hetty?"

"Well, I suppose it depends."

Hetty was grateful to have an abstract problem to think about for a moment, something other than the horrible reality of Wellington Campbell's gangrenous thumb. "More important than anything in the world, eh? You mean, something really valuable, like property?" Try as she might, she could not keep her mind from her recent dispute with her neighbor. For to Hetty, as to any member of the King family, property was life.

Wally hesitated. Property was not what he had in mind.

But Hetty was reliving this morning's accident once again. She told herself that she really must not allow this hammer business to distract her from the issue at

stake, which was, of course, her rightful claim to the
original property line.

"I'd fight for it," she said decidedly. "Once I make
up my mind that what I'm doing is right, that what I
want is right, then I fight."

"You fight. And you don't give up?" asked Wally,
nodding his head up and down, as though he had been
waiting for just such an answer.

"Give up? Me?" cried Hetty, thinking how close she
had come this morning to giving up. And all because of
an accidental tap with a hammer. "Not on your life.
When there's a goal in sight, I fight to the finish."

With a flourish she finished lacing up the skates
and held her feet out for Wally's inspection.

"There," she said triumphantly. "A perfect fit. Are
you satisfied now?"

Wally leapt up from the snow. "I'm delirious. I'm
ecstatic! A perfect, perfect fit!" he shouted. "You have made
me the happiest man on God's green earth, Hetty King!"

His energy made her feel enormously tired. If only
he would stop jumping about, or better still, go away.

"Wally, just listen to me for a moment. If you care
for me at all, then please, leave me alone and let me get
my work finished."

"If I care for you!" Wally grabbed her hand and
covered it with kisses. "Oh, poopsie-doodles, of course
I care! I care enormously, and I mean to fight, just as
you said!"

It never crossed Hetty's mind to analyze his words.

The man seemed to be departing, and that was all that mattered.

Throwing his hat in the air, Wally caught it with his head, tipped it down over one eye with his cane, winked at her and leapt on his buggy.

"See ya at the skating party, poopsie!" were the last words she heard.

Chapter Ten

Sara never slept with her drapes closed. One of the last things she did at night was to open the curtains and stand for a moment, looking out at the night.

"I feel more in touch with the day that way," she had once explained to her nanny. "I can say goodbye to it last thing at night. And I can see what kind of mood it's in, first thing in the morning."

On the day of the skating party, she awoke to a dazzle of white. As soon as she opened her eyes, she could tell there had been an overnight change, for the light that flooded her room was different. It had a brilliant, shimmering edge to it. The day, it seemed, was in a festive mood. Jumping up, she ran to the window.

In the night, snow had fallen heavily all over the Island. Towards dawn, the wind had rolled the clouds out of sight, as people roll a carpet out of the way before a party. Now the world stretched before her, polished and gleaming, silver and white, begging her to dance.

In a matter of minutes, Sara had pulled on her clothes, found her hat and coat, grabbed her skates and raced down the stairs to breakfast. She did not wish to waste a minute of the day.

"Great heavens, Sara! Anyone would think you were a racehorse, galloping downstairs, champing at the starting line, pawing the ground. Has someone entered you in a race?"

Sara shook her head. She stopped jiggling her knee and poured milk on her porridge instead.

"Civilized people do not normally wear their hats and coats at the breakfast table, you know."

Sara nodded. If she did not provoke her, Aunt Hetty would soon forget about her niece and return to her own concerns, which seemed at the moment to center on avoiding Wally Higgens.

"I can tell by my poor back it's going to freeze again." She sighed. "Perhaps I should forget about skating and stay home by the fire. What do you think, child?"

Sara opened innocent blue eyes. "Have you got cold feet, Aunt Hetty?"

"Whatever can you mean, cold feet? You think I, Hetty King, am afraid to go skating? Is that it? You think a little man like Wally Higgens scares *me*?"

Sara knew better than to reply. Placing her empty dishes in the sink, she kissed her aunt's forehead and ran out the door.

At the King farm, Felicity greeted Sara with open arms. Since Gus had invited her to the skating party, Felicity was a creature reborn. Gone were her "moods and broods," as Felix called them. Instead, she danced about the house, cooking and singing, reading stories to her baby brother and making her mother's heart light with happiness.

"I gave my hair *two* hundred strokes of the brush this morning, Sara," she confided now. "Just to be on the safe side. It usually shines after one hundred, but I wanted to be quite sure."

"It looks beautiful, Felicity. Why, it's positively sparkling. You'll turn into a snow princess before my very eyes!"

"Have a scone, Sara. I've just taken them out of the oven." Felicity pulled out a chair for her cousin and pressed her into it. The warm kitchen was filled with the steamy, comforting smell of baking, and Felicity's face shone with goodwill. Sara loved moments such as these, when they would exchange confidences openly and easily, when their small differences faded and they could concentrate on what they shared.

"I've just had breakfast," she said, reaching for a scone anyway.

"Here, try some of my rhubarb and strawberry jam with that. Then I want you to help me tie this bow in my hair." Felicity drew a scarlet ribbon from her pocket. As she did so, her eyes fell on her cousin's tangled locks. "Heavens, I hope you brought your hairbrush, Sara.

You look like you've been dragged backwards through a bush."

It was true that in her rush to enjoy the sparkling day to the full, Sara had given scant thought to her appearance. Now, her mouth full, she produced the brush from her basket and allowed her cousin to administer one hundred strokes to her yellow curls, while she helped herself to another scone.

Felix had already left to join the party of boys sweeping the snow from the Avonlea pond. He had managed to down three scones before leaving the house. Two more nestled in his coat pocket, just in case hunger struck.

"Hurry up, girls," called Janet. "Don't take all day titivating. I told Olivia I'd meet her by the pond at eleven. Isn't Hetty with you, Sara?"

"No, Aunt Janet. Mr. Higgens invited her to the skating party. He's collecting her in his buggy, so her little tootsie-wootsies won't get cold." Sara grinned at her aunt. "Poor Aunt Hetty. She's in a proper tizzy, as Nanny Louisa used to say. She's never been to the skating party with a man before. I think she's just sorry it has to be Wally Higgens!"

"I don't see that Hetty can afford to be choosy at her age," sniffed Janet. "I'm sure Mr. Higgens makes a decent living. Besides, he must be very well traveled. Run upstairs like a good girl, Sara, and see if you can find Cecily's laces. I can't think where she's put them. Last time I saw them she was using them to make a swing for her dollies."

What with one thing and another, it was approaching noon by the time the King family and Sara arrived at the pond.

Gus immediately stepped forward to claim Felicity. Wreathed in smiles, the two of them wandered off to a log, where they sat down to tie on their skates.

A throng of townsfolk in a holiday mood crowded the ice. Sara could see Aunt Hetty in the thick of it all, holding onto Wally for dear life. Her feet were completely motionless. She stood stiff and straight as an Egyptian mummy, while Mr. Higgens dragged her about the ice on her size six, quad A skates.

"Happy, sugar dumpling?" Wally beamed at Hetty as he pulled her towards the source of the music, a wind-up Victrola, lent for the occasion by Edward Lawson.

"No," snapped Hetty. "My nose is running. My feet are freezing. And I want to go home."

"I knew you'd have a good time with me."

As usual, thought Hetty sourly, the man hasn't heard a word I've said.

Indeed, Wally's mind was entirely occupied with his courtship campaign. Intent on his strategy, he now led Hetty to a bench, sat her down and bounded up to the gramophone. Lifting the needle carefully, he silenced the music. Then he bounced back towards Hetty and dragged her out onto the ice.

"What are you doing? Wally? Wally?" A nameless fear seized Hetty as Wally raised his hand for silence.

Two by two and one by one the skaters slowed down, turning to see why the music had stopped.

What now? wondered Hetty. What could the man be up to? She wished he would stop making those ridiculous flapping motions with his hands. He looked like he wanted to speak. If he wasn't careful, everybody would soon be staring at him.

"Folks! Folks! Attention, please!" called Wally.

"Shhh! Wally!" Do you want the whole of Avonlea gawking at you?" hissed Hetty. She wished she could draw away from him, but she still had those dreadful skates on her feet. If she took one step without holding onto someone or something, she would collapse on her nose, of that she was certain.

"This won't take but a minute, folks," hollered Wally. It seemed not to bother him one little bit that the eyes of everyone in town were now fixed upon him. He smiled around at the crowd, his chest swelling with happy pride, swaying a little on his feet, as though about to break into dance. Then he spoke, and what he said made Hetty pray that the ice would open up and swallow her.

"Folks," cried Wally, "the good Lord was smiling on me the day the children of Avonlea spooked my horse, Bumbles. Because one of those children ..." He smiled across the ice at Sara. "... A certain Miss Sara Stanley, led me to Rose Cottage, where I found Hetty King. The woman with the most beautiful tootsie-wootsies in the whole wide world."

An audible snigger rose from the crowd. Hetty was certain it came from Clara Potts. "Hush up at once, Wally Higgens!" she pleaded.

Wally raised his hand, the hand holding Hetty's. "She's just a little shy, folks, so I'll get right to the point. The other day I went down on my knees to her. She told me that she cared about me and she advised me to fight for what I want."

Hetty could not believe what was happening. Surely this must be a nightmare, a nightmare of the most horrendous proportions, from which she would awake soon, safe in her own little bed at Rose Cottage. She pinched her arm, willing herself to wake up. But that dreadful Yankee voice continued.

"So here goes, folks. I'm going to propose. What I want is you, Hetty King. Will you marry me?"

Hetty closed her eyes. Dear Lord, she prayed, let me wake from this terrible dream.

The voice came again. "What say we get hooked, poopsie?" it insisted. "You know, hitched?"

She could feel him fumbling for something in his pocket. A loud gasp from the crowd forced her to peek. Wally had produced a small velvet box. Snapping it open, he drew forth a gold ring set with many stones. Like all good stones, they caught the sun's rays and played with them, throwing them up in the air, juggling with them.

Hetty's eyes opened wider. Wally was holding the ring out to her. She looked up at him. Tears glistened in his eyes. His face came closer and closer. It looked solemn and happy. His arms encircled her, drawing her tightly to him. She could see the little red hairs in his mustache. Funny, she had never noticed how they matched the little red veins in his eyes. She could see his mouth. It hovered above hers. It kissed hers. The crowd broke into applause. At that moment, Hetty woke from her frozen trance and pulled away from him violently.

"No! No!" she screamed. "Get away from me, you harebrained crackpot! I'll never marry you!"

"But I love you," he replied, as though that was all that mattered. As though what she felt didn't count.

Anger boiled over in Hetty. Pulling her arm free from his, she pushed at him with all her might.

"Stop pestering me, you big lummox! " she yelled. "Don't you dare touch me ever again!"

Wally staggered backwards across the ice, his legs and arms flying in all directions. The ring, released from his grasp, flew skyward, the stones sparkling in the wintry sun. Red, green, blue, the colors arched upwards, a tiny, mobile rainbow. The crowd gasped, following its soaring flight. Then it dropped from the light. The crowd surged forward. Necks craned downwards. What had happened to the ring?

Mr. Lawson chose that moment to restart the Victrola. Once again the strains of "The Skaters' Waltz" enveloped the pond, its lilting rhythms adding to the confusion.

Chaos reigned. While some people rushed to search

for the ring, others resumed their skating. Some ran to assist Wally. Others scurried to help Hetty to her feet.

Gus Pike was one of these. He had seen Hetty push Wally Higgens away. For a second she had stood there, upright and alone, looking, to his eyes, magnificent in her anger. Then she had lost her balance, keeled over to one side and sprawled on her behind.

"I'll get her!" Gus yelled, standing up for the first time ever on skates. Thinking only of Hetty, he raced out onto the ice. His feet disappeared from under him and he fell forward onto his nose.

"Gus! Gus! Are you hurt? What happened?" Felicity skated out after him, torn between concern and laughter.

Gus lay on his stomach, feeling prickles of embarrassment break out all over his body. He forgot about Hetty. He forgot about Wally. The question that consumed him suddenly was how was he ever going to stand up? More importantly, how was he ever going to stand up without Felicity seeing that he had never skated before in his whole life? She stood there now at his side. Without raising his head, he could see her small, trim skates beside his outstretched hand.

"Gus?" she repeated. "Are you hurt?"

He could not bear to look into her face. Worry would be written on it, he knew. Yet there would also be those two tiny dimples, dancing at each corner of her mouth, waiting to burst out into a smile. He did not think he could bear to be laughed at. Not now, not lying in full public view with his nose pressed into the ice. If only he had broken a limb, then at least no one would expect him to stand up. He would be carried off the ice like a hero. But he had broken nothing, he could tell. Only his pride.

"Please. Go away, Felicity," he mumbled, keeping his head down.

"Let me help you up, why don't you? Then, if you're sure nothing's broken, we can do some figure eights together."

The borrowed skates felt like blocks of granite under his soles. He had no idea how to move on them. If he let her help him stand, she would have to prop him up, support him. She would see immediately that he was no skater. She would wonder why he had never seen fit to admit this basic fact straight out. Why in tarnation, Gus asked himself, gritting his teeth, could he not have told her the truth weeks ago? Why did this terrible, terrible pride of his keep getting in the way?

"Gus? What's wrong? You must have broken something."

"There's nothing broke. I'm fine."

"Then why don't you get up?"

"I don't want to get up. I like lying here."

"Come on, Gus. Everyone's watching. Please get up."

"Leave me alone, Felicity. I'm tired. I feel like a rest."

For another second, her skates hovered about him, then they flashed away.

He knew he had hurt her feelings. Perhaps she

would never look at him again. Gus closed his eyes. He could not lie there forever. Already skaters were gliding towards him, drawn onto the ice by the music. Taking a deep breath, he raised himself to a sitting position. He looked down at Alec King's skates, his dislike mixed with amazement. They looked so like boots. Was it any wonder he had thought skating would be as easy as walking? It was those blades that made them slippery and treacherous as a fox. He would not wear them a single moment longer. They were a sham and a pretence.

Right there on the ice, he unlaced them and ripped them off his feet. He pulled off his thick socks, too. In his bare feet, like a penitent, he stood up and walked off the pond.

From her low vantage point on the ice, Hetty had seen Gus start towards her. She had known he meant to help. But then he had stumbled and disappeared, a blur of flailing limbs. Others in the crowd had roared with laughter, both at Gus Pike's spectacular fall and at her own. Hetty was not laughing. All she wanted to do was run, run as fast as her legs would carry her back to Rose Cottage, lock the door and hide. But she could not run. She could not even stand. Every time she tried to get up, her feet slipped out from under her and she fell back again onto all fours. Very well, if she could not walk she would crawl. It was a fitting symbol of her utter humiliation. She would crawl on all fours away from this scene of pandemonium.

Snapping at those who offered assistance, dodging between legs and skates, Hetty wove her way towards the edge of the pond. She kept her head well down, hoping she was less conspicuous that way. She tried not to think how ridiculous she must look. She tried not to think about Wally Higgens and what she would like to do to him. She tried not to think at all. It was more than enough just to endure.

Wally Higgens, for his part, scrambled to his feet, clutching his head and feeling dizzy. People ran up to him, asking whether he was hurt, how he felt, whether he had found the ring, but he barely heard them. Hetty had not been pleased. Hetty had turned him down flat. Hetty had humiliated him in public. Hetty had pushed him away so hard that he had lost his balance. He had lost his balance and, worst of all, he had lost his grip on the ring.

"My ring," he whined suddenly. "A real beauty. Where is it? I paid fifty dollars for that ring, Hetty King. How could you do this to me?" So upset was Wally that he failed to notice that "ring" rhymed with "King." Ditties no longer mattered. All he could think of was that beautiful, expensive jewel, that ring on which he had pinned his hopes. It was gone, vamoosed.

Whimpering in despair, he crouched on all fours, stuck his head into a snowbank and scrabbled about. "Here, ringie-dingie," he coaxed quietly. "Come to Poppa."

Hours passed. The pale, wintry sun grew cool.

Skaters shivered and dug their hands deeper into their pockets for warmth. Visions of hot chocolate and blazing firesides stole into their heads. Small children stumbled in fatigue. They rubbed their eyes with knuckles blue from cold. Their voices rose in complaint.

Soon the pond's scratched surface stood empty, the music silent. As the sun sank and the moon rose, a passer-by might have been forgiven for thinking the Avonlea pond deserted. But no. A closer look would have revealed a pin-striped posterior poking from a snowbank over by the north side of the pond, near the village pump.

It was Wally Higgens, still searching for his ring.

Chapter Eleven

Eulalie Bugle discovered Wally Higgens much later that same night. She was on her way home from an errand which she did not describe to him. Not that he would have paid much attention. The salesman seemed completely wrapped up in his own misery. Shivering violently, he sat on a bench by the pond, his mushroom-shaped hat beside him.

"Gracious me, can it be Mr. Higgens?" enquired Eulalie, peering at him through the shadows.

"My jewel," he said, looking up at the sound of her voice. "I've lost her."

Mrs. Bugle had attended the skating party earlier

that day. Along with almost the entire population of Avonlea, she had witnessed what had transpired between Hetty King and Wally Higgens. She wondered now whether Wally was referring to Hetty or the ring. That he had lost both forever she had no doubt.

"You'll catch your death of cold, if you keep sitting there, Mr. Higgens," she said, pulling him to his feet. "You should be in bed with a hot drink. Come along with me now, I'll be passing by your boarding house on my way home."

Without another word, Wally Higgens went along with her. She was a large woman and there was something comforting about her bulk. He felt sheltered beside her, like a lost, sail-tattered ship that has found a safe port out of the storm. Together they walked the remaining distance between the pond and Mrs. Biggins's boarding house.

"If you're still feeling poorly in the morning, stop by Elvira Lawson at the store. She'll see you right."

Before he could thank her, she had pulled Myrtle Biggins's bell and was gone.

Wally was still shivering when he awoke the next morning. Pulling on his boots with shaking hands, he made his way over to Lawson's store. He was greeted like a conquering hero as soon as he entered.

"My poor dear man. Here, let me take your coat. A nice hot cup of tea for Mr. Higgens, Edward, quickly! " Elvira hurried to the back of the store and returned with a blanket. "Here, wrap this round you at once and go sit by that fire."

"Would you look at the state of him?" clucked Rachel Lynde to Clara Potts. "He looks like he's been to hell and back, the poor soul."

"It's a crying shame, that's what," sighed Archie Gillis, slapping Wally on the back sympathetically and moving away from the fire, so Wally could draw closer. Bert MacKay shook Wally's hand and solemnly offered his condolences.

"There, now, get this down you," said Elvira, taking the cup of steaming tea from her husband's hand and carrying it to Wally. "Drink this before you say another word."

As yet, Wally had said nothing. But the warmth of their sympathy thawed his frozen heart. He drew the blanket around him and felt his shivering abate.

"How could such a thing happen?" Elvira asked the store in general. "And in Avonlea, of all places?"

"Anything's possible, where Hetty King's concerned," said Archie darkly.

At the mention of Hetty's name, Wally winced. The hand carrying the cup to his lips faltered.

"Hetty King has been a thorn in the side of many before you, Mr. Higgens," Rachel informed him.

"Such a fine, perceptive man," sighed Clara Potts, remembering Wally's insight into her artistic nature. "So sensitive. It's a wonder he didn't read her character better."

Wally's eyes filled up with tears. "But her feet," he whispered. "How could I have misjudged her so?"

"Mistakes are what we learn by." Rachel patted him bracingly on the shoulder. "What you must do now is stand up to her."

"Exactly," agreed Clara. "Why should she get away with humiliating decent souls in front of everyone?" It seemed to have slipped Clara's mind entirely that her laughter had been loudest of all, as Hetty and Wally lay sprawled on the ice.

"She just uses people for her own ends," said Archie, remembering an old grievance. "Somebody ought to take her down a peg or two."

Rachel narrowed her eyes. "I saw her riding up there on your buggy, Mr. Higgens. With my own two eyes. She was leading you on shamelessly."

Wally's trembling began again. That journey to Carmody with Hetty had been one of the happiest moments in his life. Since yesterday, it had become one of his saddest memories. Tears welled in his eyes.

"Put her in her place. That's what you should do," advised Bert MacKay.

"Show her what's what. That's what," urged Rachel.

The tears trickled down his tired face and took refuge in his mustache. He wiped them away with a shaking hand. "Those lovely little tootsies," he moaned.

"May I suggest what I think is a rather creative solution?" Clara Potts blushed becomingly. "I'm sure it would help you feel better, Mr. Higgens."

Sitting down beside him, she took out her gold-plated pencil, an anniversary gift from her husband. For years it had languished in an old jar on the kitchen shelf, rescued only when a shopping list or a note became necessary. But ever since Mr. Higgens had seen into her very soul and pronounced her an artist, she had taken to carrying it with her everywhere she went. Now it gleamed in the firelight as she wrote down several key words, concentrating on spelling them correctly. "Solicitor" was one. "Breach of promise" came next.

Wally Higgens listened carefully to the plan as outlined by Clara Potts. It was not a plan he would ever have dreamed up himself, for he was not a malicious man. But then, never in his whole life had he been involved in such a calamity.

It seemed to Hetty that the dark clouds of humiliation bunched above her head were growing thicker and more oppressive by the hour. They had been gathering ever since Mr. Wally Higgens had first knocked on her door. Yesterday's public disgrace at the pond had been like a shaft of lightning, and she saw that worse would surely follow. The heavens had not yet finished with her.

"Oh the shabe, the shabe!" she groaned now, as she sat by the kitchen table inhaling hot steam from the basin in front of her, trying to clear the dreadful cold that she had caught at the pond. "It beggars description, Sara. Why, I'be neber felt so hubiliated id by whole life."

Sara nodded soothingly. Aunt Hetty's blocked

sinuses made it hard to follow anything she said. Far better merely to pretend to understand the one-sided conversation. She poured more hot water from the heavy kettle into the basin, to which her aunt had previously added a few drops of eucalyptus oil.

Once again, Aunt Hetty's mournful face disappeared under the towel. The hot, aromatic steam forced itself into her nostrils, her eyes, her throat. She inhaled deeply. A sense of doom pervaded her whole being. The storm had not yet broken, of that she felt sure. The worst was yet to come. The unfairness of it all overcame her. She was not to blame. She had certainly not led Wally on. He had misinterpreted her meaning. Sputtering and gasping she emerged from under the towel.

"I neber said I lobed hib, Sara. Neber. I neber eben said I cared about hib. What I said was, 'If you care for be ...'"

"Of course, Aunt Hetty."

The steam mingled with tears on Aunt Hetty's face. "He took it the wrog way. That's what happened. And now it's all a bonstrous bix-up!"

Just how monstrous the mix-up was became clear that same evening when a loud knocking sounded on the door of Rose Cottage. Hetty turned pale and dropped her soup spoon with a clatter.

"If it's hib, tell hib I'b not hobe. I'b gone to China."

Olivia rose from the table with a sigh. She had chores to do at home, yet she did not like to leave Hetty alone, given her mood, and Sara was visiting with her cousins at the King farm. As dusk fell, Olivia had cooked a light supper, concerned that her sister's mournfulness seemed to deepen rather than lift as the day wore on.

Olivia returned from the front door holding a large brown envelope.

"Whassat?" hissed Hetty, eyeing the flat package as though it were about to explode. "Did HE brig it?"

"That wasn't Mr. Higgens, Hetty. It was a messenger from our solicitor's office in Carmody. It's addressed to you."

Using her dinner knife as a letter opener, Hetty slit the envelope. Two documents fell out. Before unfolding them, she glanced skyward, straightening her back. The storm had reached its peak. She recognized it. As soon as she opened these documents, it would break over her head. Her heart clapped like thunder in her ears. She read aloud.

"'Biss Hetty Kigg is hereby sued by Bister Wellington Cabbell of Avonlea for two hundred and fifty dollars for intent to cobbit grievous bodily harb and assault with a dangerous weapon.'"

Olivia gasped.

Hetty eyed her. "The worst is not yet over, Olivia. Brace yourself." Picking up the second document, she resumed. "'Biss Hetty Kigg is hereby sued by Wally Higgens of Chicago for two hundred and fifty dollars for breach of probise and public ebbarrassbent. An additional fifty dollars is claibed for the loss of an engagebent rigg.'"

"What in heaven's name will you do, Hetty?"

Hetty stood up, clutching the table, her knuckles white with effort. Her body felt buffeted and wracked by the storm. She had to struggle to stand upright. The world had grown dark before her eyes. The beat of her heart almost deafened her. She wanted to cringe and hide her head.

"I shall seek shelter, of course," she cried, raising her voice over the howl in her head. "Always the wisest course in a storb. I shall wait it out in by bed."

"You can't go to bed, Hetty. Not now. You must be up and doing. You can't let these men sue you like this. You must fight!"

Hetty smiled wearily. Launching herself from the table, she set her course for the door, her body swaying and pitching. "Bed!" she called, and her voice came to Olivia's ears faint and storm-tossed, as though carried to her on the wind.

For the rest of that evening and all the next day, Hetty lay face down on her bed, her head tucked under her pillow. She paid no attention to Olivia's entreaties. Nor did she seem to hear Sara and Felicity, who stood by her door for hours, murmuring what they hoped were words of encouragement.

Finally, towards evening of the following day, she lifted the pillow, twisted her head around and gazed blearily about her. On a branch outside her window a small bird sang. Its thin, reedy chirping attracted her attention. She turned over onto her back. The bird continued to sing, as though in defiance of the cold and approaching dark. Hetty took a deep breath. There were no other sounds. The pounding of her heart had quieted. Her body, though exhausted, was in one piece. Her sinuses had cleared.

Turning on her pillow, she attacked it fiercely, pummelling it into shape. Then she propped herself against it, closing her eyes and folding her arms.

"Talk to her, girls, talk to her. I'll go make tea!" Olivia scurried downstairs, having read the signs correctly. Hetty would survive.

"How are you feeling, Aunt Hetty?" asked Sara. Both girls entered the room cautiously. They watched their aunt intently, afraid she might at any moment return to her hiding place under the pillow.

Hetty did not open her eyes. "Such humiliation is hard to endure, children. No one in the King family has ever been sued before. Yet I must suffer the shame of being sued twice in one day!" She turned her head away. "Under such circumstances, it's hard for a body to face the world."

Sara's patience with her aunt had reached its limit. What was the use of moaning about humiliation and shame? She was sick of the words.

"Perhaps you should just pay them each two hundred and fifty dollars, and have done with it," she said suddenly. "You'd have to pay Wally three hundred, of course, to make up for the price of the ring. That would make a total of five hundred and fifty dollars."

Her aunt's eyes snapped open. "I'll do nothing of the kind!"

Sara smiled. "That sounds more like you, Aunt Hetty."

Her aunt lifted a pale hand and felt her hair, as though expecting to find it in disarray. "I've no idea what to do any more," she mumbled. "I'm so confused."

"You could explain to Wally what you really meant."

Hetty shook her head. "Events have developed far beyond the stage of explanations, Sara, I'm afraid."

Felicity fiddled with the knob of her aunt's glass powder jar on the dresser. A story she had read in the *Family Guide* came back to her. "Perhaps Mr. Higgens might drop his lawsuit if he thought you were already promised to another man," she suggested slowly.

Hetty glared at her. "Sounds like romantic twaddle from some second-rate magazine."

Felicity raised the powder puff and dabbed it on her nose. Aunt Hetty had never approved of the *Family Guide*, although once or twice Felicity had caught her sneaking a look at its pages.

"I don't remember the story exactly," she continued, thinking back. "It had something to do with this woman who wanted to remain unmarried. I can't think why. But she did. Anyway, she realized that some men don't always understand this—you know, the desire to remain single. So she pretended to be engaged to someone else in order to stay free."

Felicity considered the effect of the powder in the mirror. It made her look like a clown. Her aunt and her cousin were both staring at her. She rubbed it hastily from her nose.

"I suppose that's a clever idea," Sara said slowly, thinking it over. "It shows a good understanding of human nature. Only, what a shame she had to lie about something like that."

Hetty was gazing at Felicity with an expression akin to respect. "Felicity King," she cried, jumping out of bed. "I do believe you've hit on the solution. Quickly girls, find me my new hat, the one with the cherries on it. Oh, yes, and that cunning little muff. Hurry now. Bring them down to me in the kitchen. I must just go whip up something scrumptious for Wellington Campbell!"

Chapter Twelve

Wellington Campbell squinted through the dusty glass of his front door. Could that be Hetty King standing outside? Surely not. Whoever it was, she was wearing a decidedly glamorous hat with red objects dangling from it. More to the point, she was holding what appeared to be a cake. A heady aroma of chocolate, cinnamon and baked plum reached him even through the thick glass.

Never in all the years Wellington Campbell had lived near Rose Cottage had Hetty King ever brought him a single muffin, not to speak of a cake. Yet she was renowned throughout the Island for her baking. Her butter tarts were legendary. Such culinary meanness rankled. He knew she knew he was a bachelor. She must have guessed he could barely boil an egg that didn't come out hard as the hobs of hell. She must have suspected he would have welcomed the odd upside-down cake or apple tart from time to time. In short, Wellington Campbell blamed Hetty for the fact that they were neighbors only in geography and not in spirit. That he himself might have done something to contribute to the spirit of neighborliness had never occurred to him.

"Who is it?" he called out now, sounding as ungracious as he felt.

"It's I, Hetty King, your neighbor."

As he opened the door, Hetty blushed the shade of the cherries trimming her hat.

Wellington Campbell wondered if he needed spectacles. It certainly sounded like the voice of Hetty King. Yet the woman standing before him in her elaborate hat and matching muff looked, well, quite frankly, much too attractive to be his old neighbor.

"I brought this for you," she said now, holding out her peace offering. "It's a freshly baked plum cake. May I come in?"

Spectacles or no spectacles, that plum cake looked perfect. His mouth watered. His stomach pleaded.

"If you must," he said grumpily and stepped back for her to enter.

"I'll just put the kettle on for tea, shall I?" She smiled, taking over. In the wink of an eye she had drawn a table up to the fire, set it with his best china, warmed the pot and made the tea. She had even managed, God knows how, to unearth the pastry forks his mother had wrapped in green baize years ago and hidden in the bottom drawer of the dining room cabinet.

"I wanted to tell you how badly I feel about your poor thumb," she said, slicing into the plum cake. "Although I'm very glad to see that you decided against amputation."

Had she said "amputation"? The unfortunate woman must be mad as a March hare! Still, deranged or not, she seemed to be able to cook. Better not provoke her, at least, not until he had sampled the cake. He tried to keep his tone mild.

"I hope you dinna imagine you can bribe me with cake into giving up my suit," he responded, accepting the generous slice she handed him. "This thumb of mine's fairly killing me, and it's all your fault, Hetty King."

"I just wish I could think of something to make up for what I've done." Hetty gazed at him contritely.

Why had he never noticed those dark eyes before? Perhaps it was her hat, which was trimmed with a dark veil, that complemented the eyes, adding to their mystery. Wellington shifted in his seat. He had always enjoyed a good mystery. The cake was confoundedly good too—light, moist, perfectly spiced. He contemplated sneaking another slice while her back was turned. But she was looking at him now, the somber eyes suddenly brightening, as though struck by an idea.

"I know," she suggested. "Why don't we agree to a compromise over our little property squabble?"

Did he need a hearing aid as well as spectacles?

"You mean," he asked incredulously. "You mean, you'd hand over part of your land to me, because you hit my thumb with a wee hammer?"

"Yes and no, Mr. Campbell. There's one other little matter I have to settle first."

"What wee matter would that be?"

Hetty lowered her eyes. "It seems that I am also being sued by a certain Mr. Higgens from Chicago, for breach of promise."

Breach of promise? This particular book could certainly not be judged by its cover. "What does breach of promise have to do with my thumb?"

"Simply this," she replied, fiddling with the cake knife. "I do not wish to marry Mr. Higgens. Therefore, I need you to pose as my fiancé."

Wellington Campbell almost choked on his last bite of cake. "You need me to WHAT?"

"I need you to pretend that we are engaged to be married. That we've been engaged for years. Seeing that I am spoken for, Mr. Higgens will then withdraw his suit."

Hetty spoke with more confidence than she felt. She did not dare think what might happen if Wally refused to behave as planned.

Wellington Campbell leaned forward, drew the knife from Hetty's nervous fingers, cut himself a huge slice of cake and popped the whole thing into his mouth. He chewed thoughtfully for a while. There was no denying the cake was a masterpiece. Anyone who could bake like that deserved a second chance. Besides, what she was suggesting could work out to his advantage.

"If I agree to pose in this way, and this man then withdraws, the land's mine, is that what you're proposing?"

Hetty nodded.

An old familiar dread, the dread of being trapped into matrimony, made Wellington Campbell shiver suddenly. He drew closer to the fire.

"I have your word this arrangement between us wouldna go any further? It would remain, er, strictly a business matter?"

Hetty stood up. "Believe me, Mr. Campbell, I am not the kind of woman who seeks a husband at any cost. No, once Wally, I mean, Mr. Higgens has realized his mistake and returned to Chicago, then you will drop your assault charge, of course. And I, why, I'll agree to renegotiate our property line."

Wellington Campbell wiped the crumbs from his chin and shirt with one of the linen napkins Hetty had found in the cedar chest in the hall. It had been many years since he had enjoyed tea in front of the fire like this. He stood up and held out his hand to her.

"Allow me to congratulate you on your engagement, Miss King," he said. There was a rare twinkle in his eye. "You have shown rare insight in your choice of suitor."

Hetty took the proffered hand and shook it firmly up and down, causing Wellington Campbell to double over in sudden pain. In her eagerness she had clasped the whole hand, including his injured thumb!

Chapter Thirteen

No trace of anger or hurt appeared on the face of Wellington Campbell the next morning, however, when he stepped into Mr. Lawson's store bearing Hetty King on his arm. Indeed, thoughts of the extra land he was about to acquire caused him to straighten his shoulders and glance about him with eager eyes.

Hetty, too, seemed to glow, but whether it was from delight in her neighbor's company or nerves over what was about to transpire must be left for the reader to judge.

A hush fell over the assembled townsfolk as the pair entered. Seeing them, Rachel Lynde was reminded of the first time she had laid eyes on Wally Higgens. At that time he had seemed to bring the sun with him, so radiant was his smile. Now the light seemed to have shifted to Hetty King and her neighbor, while Wally Higgens walked in shadow. Gone was his warm, happy smile, his bouncing step.

As Hetty and Wellington advanced, Wally retreated. Without once taking his eyes off Hetty, he slouched backwards until he was jammed up against the shop counter.

"Wh-who? Wh-wha-what?" he asked, pointing at Wellington Campbell. Beads of perspiration stood out on his forehead.

Hetty was smiling relentlessly. "I don't believe you've met my fiancé, Wellington Campbell, have you, Wally?" She switched her attention to her neighbor, gazing into his eyes. "Welly," she purred, "meet Wally, Wally Higgens."

Tears sprang to Wally's eyes. "He's your what?" he whispered. "What did you say he was?"

"My fiancé," repeated Hetty. "My betrothed. My affianced love. Tell Wally, Welly."

Wellington Campbell continued to gaze at Hetty. He was beginning to enjoy himself enormously. "We've been engaged for years." He smiled down at her. "In secret, of course."

Rachel gave a loud, equine snort. "Hogwash! A load of hogwash!"

Hetty tore her eyes away from Wellington to flash them at Rachel. "You don't know everything about me, Rachel Lynde. You certainly know nothing about my private life."

Wally crouched against the counter. He seemed utterly crushed. "Why didn't you tell me, sweetcakes?" he whispered. "You never mentioned a Wellington. Never ever. You accepted the candies and the skates. And all the time you were engaged to a guy ..." His voice cracked. "To a guy low enough to be named after cheap waterproof boots!"

Wellington Campbell bristled. "I'll have you know I was named after the Duke of Wellington, laddie. The Iron Duke."

"Iron, ha! Rubber, more likely!"

Wally stood up straight. He blinked back his tears. A man could only be pushed so far, and no farther.

At that moment Clara Potts poked him with her gold-plated pencil. "Don't just stand there," she urged. "Do something!"

"Yes," hissed Rachel. "You can't let them get away with it."

"All right," answered Wally, suddenly resolved. He turned to Hetty. "I'll do something. I will. I will. I'll fight for you, poopsie. Just like you said I should." Tearing his mittens out of his pocket, he flung them at Wellington's feet. "I challenge you to a duel, Mr. Wellington Boots."

A look of horror crossed Wellington Campbell's face. A duel! No such item had been included in his and Miss King's little arrangement.

"Now just a minute, laddie," he objected. "You listen to me." For the umpteenth time he wished he had insisted on a written agreement. These verbal contracts could become very messy, very messy indeed. But no one was listening. The whole store seemed seized with the fever of battle.

"I'll be your second, Mr. Higgens," volunteered Rachel, throwing herself into the spirit of the thing.

Wellington Campbell felt himself seized from behind and steered out into the street, where Wally Higgens had already stripped off his coat and was rolling up his sleeves. All the little salesman's spirit had returned in a rush. Rising on his toes, he executed a couple of dance-like steps around his opponent.

"Put 'em up, smelly ol' Welly!" he taunted. "Face me if you dare! Galoshes! Rubbers! Wellington boots! Ha! What kind of a name is that for a fella?"

Such insults were too much for Wellington Campbell. Hearing some upstart salesman from Chicago mock the name of which he was inordinately proud was more than he could bear. He removed his hat.

"Very well, Mr. Higgens," he said, with as much dignity as he could muster. "I accept your challenge."

A great cheer went up. The circle of onlookers tightened around the two men.

Hetty found herself outside the circle, trying to get in. "Stop this, at once, Wellington!" she cried. "This wasn't what I wanted!" But all eyes and ears were fixed on Wally and Welly as they danced around each other, their fists raised.

"Good heavens, Hetty!" Olivia came dashing up to

her sister. "Put an end to this at once. This is no way to solve an argument!"

"I tried," whispered Hetty, her eyes filled with horror. "But nobody listens to me."

"Duck and bob and weave, Wally," roared Rachel Lynde, her cheeks red with excitement.

"That Wellington Campbell's soft as mush!" cried Bert MacKay. "You've nothing to worry about at all, Wally."

All of a sudden the two men leapt at each other like tigers. So strong was the impetus of the attack that they lost their balance. Missing each other completely, they reeled about, ending up in a heap on the sidewalk, yards apart. Wally's trousers were covered with snow. Wellington's shirt was all askew.

Jumping to their feet they grabbed each other and hung on grimly, neither one able to figure out quite what to do next.

"Separate them!" yelled Archie Gillis. "They ain't supposed to cling on like that."

As though specifically summoned, Hetty stepped into the fray. She would save the day. She would separate these two idiotic men, who should know better than to forget the old truth that brains are always better than brawn. Throwing her arms around Wally, she tried to pull him away from Wellington. But he seemed stuck fast. She yanked at Wellington's coat. All to no avail. Finally, on an instinct, without having fully worked out what she intended to do, she raised her heavy shopping basket. It came crashing down on Wellington's head. For a second he stood immobile, still clinging to Wally. Then his arms dropped to his side. He spun around and fell without a word to the ground.

Released from Wellington's hold, Wally aimed a powerful swing at his antagonist, just as Wellington slipped to the sidewalk. Missing its aim, Wally's arm swung around, almost choking Wally himself. He gasped, staggered backwards and fell with a huge crash through the front window of Lawson's store.

As Hetty saw Wellington sink silently to earth, the enormity of what she had done rose up inside her. She saw clearly that in seeking to wriggle out of her problems through deceit, she had harmed not only herself, but others as well. She fell to her knees beside her unconscious neighbor, lifting his head onto her lap.

"Wellington! Speak to me!" she cried. "Fetch the doctor someone! Quickly! Oh what have I done? What have I done?"

Wally Higgens brushed the glass from his clothes, felt around for his spectacles and sat up. His neck felt a trifle sore, but other than that, he was unharmed. Peering out from the broken window, he saw a sight that made his damaged heart almost break.

Framed by the shattered glass, Hetty King bent, a ministering angel, over the prostrate form of Wellington Campbell. She was crying. Tears streamed down her thin cheeks as she cradled her neighbor's head in her lap. If Wally had previously doubted Hetty's attachment to

Wellington, he could doubt it no longer. Grief was etched in her every feature. The sight was more than Wally could bear. Standing up, he rescued his hat from under a mound of glass and tiptoed away from the scene.

Chapter Fourteen

Gus Pike could see them coming. He stood by the lighthouse door, watching Sara and Felix climb the hill towards him. He was not in the mood for visitors. Since the disaster at the pond, he had not ventured out into the village. There was plenty of work to be done at the lighthouse anyway. Besides, he felt safe here. No one would laugh at him or point fingers or make jokes about fellas who couldn't stand up without falling over.

He tried not to worry about Felicity, but she kept popping into his head when he least expected it. He would be mending a net and there her face would be in one of the squares—not saying anything, just looking at him, in a reproachful kind of way. He'd turn to climb the lighthouse stairs and she'd appear on the landing, her back turned to him, one foot tapping the floor quietly, as though waiting for him to speak.

The trouble was, he didn't know what to say. If he wanted to speak plainly and honestly, he would have to start way back at the beginning, at his mother's death, perhaps. And that would take a whole lot of talking. How could a girl like Felicity King, who had never experienced a moment of need or neglect, understand what life was like for Gus Pike, who had never known anything else? Sometimes he feared the huge gap between them could never be bridged. He would need thousands, no, millions of words before he could hope to build a path across to her, where they could both meet and understand each other.

Sometimes he wondered whether he should just give up. In some ways it would be so much easier if he left Avonlea altogether, if he tried to stop thinking about Felicity, if he drove her from his mind. After all, they were both still very young. It would be years before she could even think of marrying.

Marrying. A little, self-mocking smile tugged at Gus's mouth. There was the whole problem in a nutshell. What made him think he, Gus Pike, stood even the remotest chance of marrying someone like Felicity King? She was a dream, an unreachable, outrageous dream. Yet without that dream, he found it difficult to breathe in and out, to go to work each morning or to continue his studies. She was his sun. Without her, he would live in darkness.

"Gus," called Sara, breasting the hill, breaking into his reverie. "Why haven't you been to see us? Where've you been hiding?"

Gus sighed and went to meet them, trying to shake off the feeling of hopelessness that seemed to follow at his heels these days like a hungry stray.

Felix had brought some cookies, baked by Felicity. Gus stared at them. She was always so thoughtful, so generous. Even now, when she probably felt like strangling him, she could make a kind, simple gesture like baking cookies.

"Felicity says the skating party was one of the most embarrassing moments of her life," said Felix, as though reading Gus's mind.

"Hush up, Felix," said Sara, who had sensed Gus's mood as he greeted them.

Felix reached for his third cookie. "Well, you did look a hoot, Gus, crashing down like that and then lying there for ages like a beached whale! I was in stitches."

"Those cookies were meant for Gus, Felix, so you can stop stuffing them in your mouth this minute," snapped Sara, wrapping the cookies back up and tucking them into Gus's pocket.

Gus's face had darkened. Turning away from them, he walked back up to the base of the lighthouse, where he searched through a clutter of supplies. When he turned back, he was holding up Uncle Alec's skates by their laces.

"You can return these to your uncle, Sara," he said now. "I won't have no more use of 'em."

Felix reached to take the skates, but Sara stopped him. Instinctively, she felt that Gus had reached a crossroads in his life. One road wended away from them— away from Avonlea, away from his friends, away from school and away from Felicity. Everything about him suggested that his feet were bent in that direction. She noted the slack shoulders, the sadness in his eyes. He had not changed his shirt since the skating party. Once crisp and white, it now looked grubby and rumpled. His hair was uncombed, his hands stained from work. She knew Gus to be fastidious about his appearance, whenever possible. His clothes, although never new, were always clean. He darned them himself. He was hard-working, courageous, honest. She liked him more than she could say, and she did not want him to go.

Taking the skates from Gus's outstretched hand, she dropped them on the ground like a challenge. Her blue eyes looked hard.

"I never thought you were a quitter, Gus," she said. "I never thought you'd let your pride get the better of you. I never thought you'd give up and walk away." Turning her back on him, she ran down the hill, not even waiting for Felix.

For a long time Gus stood where they had left him, watching them disappear from sight. Then, leaving the skates where they lay, he went into the lighthouse and closed the door.

The back door of the King farmhouse opened and Felicity tiptoed out. Over her arm she carried her skates. All her chores were done, and what she wanted most of all now was to be alone. If she hurried, she would have an hour to herself before supper.

She ran lightly across the yard and through the gate leading to the pond, which stood frozen and inviting at the bottom of the lower meadow. Sitting on the fence, she hurriedly pulled on her skates and stepped out onto the ice. It felt firm under her blades. Inhaling deeply, she closed her eyes, taking deep, gliding strides, trying to clear her mind of everything but what was important. Gus was important. She must try to sweep away the rest—the feeling of humiliation, the resentment at his silence, at his pride, at his refusal to reveal his feelings.

Once again, the wonder of it all swept Felicity. As a young girl, she had felt convinced of the importance of many things—how to speak, how to dress, how to sew, how to cook, how to bake, how to learn. She had worked hard at her self-appointed tasks, and she had mastered most of them. But she saw now that each task had been concrete, practical, something with borders that were easy to define. What she was coming up against now were the larger, more baffling elements of life. These, she realized, were far more important and had hardly any borders at all. It was the way she felt about Gus that had truly expanded Felicity's mind. Because of him, she had become aware of the terrible complexities of life, and its startling simplicity.

A little wind had arisen, sending tremors through the rushes by the edge of the pond. Felicity skated effortlessly, her mind on Gus.

Gus said "I ain't" instead of "I am not," although

recently he had been trying hard to correct his grammar, staying behind after school with Aunt Hetty. Felicity had always thought bad grammar one of the things she could least abide. Yet placed beside the things she admired in Gus, she saw it as a small, practical problem, one that could be resolved, given time and the right frame of mind. What she admired in Gus—his kindness, his gentleness, his unfailing courage—were more elusive qualities. These she couldn't change or touch, but they made her happy.

The worried expression she had worn since the skating party dissolved. She felt a lightness within her. If you could just keep in mind what was important, the little things eventually fell into place and stopped bothering you. Opening her eyes, she bent low over the ice, executing three figure eights in a row. Her frozen breath danced ahead of her. The air was clean and sharp with cold. She felt blessed.

As she came around by the fence for the third time, she saw a familiar figure sitting there.

"Gus!" she exclaimed.

Seeing the radiance of her smile, Gus felt his heart sing. All his thoughts of leaving Avonlea, of forgetting Felicity, vanished in a surge of happiness. As she glided up to him, he began pulling on Uncle Alec's skates.

"I was thinkin' of givin' 'em back," he said, as he tied up the laces.

"You don't have to do that, Gus. Father doesn't use them any more."

"I know. I didn't come to give 'em back. I come to apologize. I should've told you the truth in the first place."

"I want you to tell me the truth always."

He took a deep breath. "I've no money to buy skates. I never learnt to skate in the first place. I got two left feet. An' more pride than brains."

"Is that all?"

"It's enough to be goin' on with."

"I would've been happy to give you lessons, Gus. You should've seen me when I first started to skate. I was so clumsy!"

He looked at her. Her cheeks were flushed from the cold and the exercise. Her eyes glowed. He wanted to push back the curls of hair that had slipped out from under her hood. He wanted to touch the dimples dancing at the corners of her mouth.

"You could never be clumsy, Felicity," was all he said.

His look and words made Felicity's heart miss a beat. Her knees felt like water. He made her feel shy and proud, happy and sad. There were no borders to the way she felt about Gus Pike. He was part of a vast, unfathomable mystery she was just beginning to understand.

She held out her hand. "Come on, let me give you your first lesson."

Chapter Fifteen

Eulalie Bugle shifted her weight from her left foot to her right. She had been standing outside Mrs. Biggins's boarding house since six o'clock that morning, with the wind nipping at her ankles. She was cold and cranky and would have sold her soul for a cup of hot, sweet coffee. She could have knocked on the door and asked for permission to wait inside, but she had no desire to wake up Mrs. Biggins. Mrs. Biggins was a notorious busybody, and Eulalie did not want her to know her business. Eulalie's mission was to speak to Wally Higgens. To him alone would she unburden herself.

Darkness still lay over Avonlea, although if she looked east, Mrs. Bugle could see a fringe of pale gray bordering the black curtain of night. Avonlea, always so familiar, so taken for granted, seemed strange to her now. For the first time, she wondered about other people's lives. Looking at the closed doors, at the dark, curtained windows that stared out on the street like blank eyes, she perceived dimly that even those she thought she knew, her neighbors and friends, had secrets, just as she did.

There was a stirring inside the boarding house. Light shone from one of the top bedrooms. She prayed it was Mr. Higgens getting dressed. He had to be out on the road early, she knew. He had told Rachel Lynde of a business appointment in Charlottetown, and no doubt there were other calls to make along the way.

After a while she heard the creak of the staircase and heavy footsteps descending. The front door opened and Wally Higgens stepped out, holding one of his sample cases.

"Mr. Higgens," she hissed, looming at him from out of the darkness. "I must speak to you."

Wally put down his sample case. He recognized her as the lady with the bunions. He had read her feet. Another more recent memory of her imposed itself on the first. This memory was darker, shaded with confusion and sadness. It was she who had found him sitting in misery on the bench by the pond the night of the skating party. She had been kind to him.

"What can I do for you, ma'am?" he asked now. He kept his voice low. Something about the way she looked and moved told him she did not want anyone to know she was there.

Eulalie had not realized how nervous she was until it came time for her to speak. Her mouth felt so dry, she could hardly frame the words. Besides, she did not know what words to use.

"Could we ... could we sit ... just for a moment? I know, that bench by the pond, we could sit there."

Wally stowed his sample case inside Mrs. Biggins's front door and allowed himself to be led towards the pond. He had no desire to revisit the place that he associated with calamity, for that was how he now thought of his courting of Hetty King. But he was a kind man and wise enough to know that no woman waits outside a man's boarding house in the cold of dawn unless she feels compelled to do so.

"I got a feeling in my tootsie-wootsies something's troubling you, ma'am," he said as soon as they sat down. "Why don't you tell me what it is?"

Eulalie twiddled the clasp of her purse, not looking at him. "It's really nothing to do with you, Mr. Higgens. But I don't know who else to tell, see?"

"Think of me as an ear, Mrs. ...?"

"Never mind my name, if you don't mind. Now, there are two reasons for my thinking I can talk to you, Mr. Higgens."

"And what might they be?"

"Well, the first is, that day you looked at my corns and my bunions, you saw something about me straightaway that nobody else knows. And the second is, you'll be going away this morning and not coming back. Am I right there, Mr. Higgens?"

"You're certainly right there, ma'am. Wally Higgens will not be returning to this particular burg, not if he can help it."

Eulalie Bugle tightened her grasp on her purse and began. "That time you saw my corns, Mr. Higgens, you mentioned worries and woes."

"A cramped, pinched personality," he murmured. "That's often what bunions and corns indicate. Only it ain't always so. Not in every case."

"But it *is* so in mine. You see, Mr. Higgens, ever

since my Cornelia left home to be married, I've been like a woman possessed."

"Possessed, ma'am?" He shifted away from her slightly. "In what way?"

Eulalie's body heaved. The sobs seemed to swell up from her boots. "I've been so unhappy, Mr. Higgens. I couldn't get used to my Corny not being there. The house felt so empty, see? Like everywhere I turned I saw little reminders of her. Things she'd made, or something she'd said or done. Right there in that corner by the fire. Or over by the curtains, near my sewing-basket. Or out where we keep the milking stool."

She stopped, choked by sobs. Her hands, small for such a big woman, groped at the clasp on her purse, wrenched it open and fumbled for her handkerchief.

Wally Higgens patted her shoulder awkwardly. "There, there now. Don't take on so. Every mother feels the same way when her children leave home."

"Yes, but not every mother sinks to *stealing*!"

He sat up straight. "Stealing?"

She abandoned the search for her handkerchief. "Stealing," she repeated dully, after a sniff or two. "I don't know what comes over me. I'll be in this store or that, here or in Carmody, sometimes even in Charlottetown. And when I come home I find things in my basket. Things I never meant to take. Things I don't even *need*." Her voice had risen to a wail. The tears streamed unchecked down her cheeks. "I never thought I'd ever have to say this, Mr. Higgens, but I've been no better than a common thief!"

Taking his clean handkerchief from his breast pocket, he handed it to her. "Now I'd say that all depends, ma'am," he said slowly. "It all depends on what you do about it."

"Why, I take the things back, of course! I take them back straightaway. But just imagine how difficult it can be, trying to put something back that you shouldn't have touched in the first place! It's mortifying, that's what it is, absolutely mortifying."

She rocked back and forth on the bench in silence for a moment, holding his handkerchief over her eyes, as though trying to shield them from such agonizing memories. Then she removed it to plead with him. "Advise me, Mr. Higgens. Tell me what to do. I feel so wretched."

Wally Higgens looked out over the frozen pond. Dawn had tiptoed up on them as they were talking. The sun was still in hiding, but a mysterious, pearly light touched the surface of things. The pond glowed with a dim radiance. He cast his mind back to his own youth. He remembered how effortlessly he and his brothers had left home. They were like caterpillars, he thought, shucking off old skins without a thought, except for how it would feel to fly. Yet what else could they do? Leaving home and parents had seemed the most natural thing in the world at the time. Could they have done it differently? he wondered. Not for one moment had they considered how their parents might feel. Yet his mother, a fat, jolly woman, had never complained. She had busied herself with countless causes, charities and bake sales. She had seemed to cope.

"As long as you don't mean to steal what you steal, as long as you bring it all back, I don't think you can call yourself a regular, common or garden-variety thief," he said at last.

"I certainly feel like one!" she whispered. Rivulets of tears splashed down her several chins like tiny waterfalls and disappeared under her collar. His handkerchief was drenched.

"You've got to stop going into stores. That's what you've got to do, ma'am. Not forever, of course. Only till you got this little problem of yours licked. Get your hubby to do the shopping. You got a hubby, aint you?"

She nodded. The thought of Alfred wielding a shopping basket made her smile through her tears. But come to think of it, Alfred had a good eye for bargains. Who could say? Maybe he'd make a better shopper than she ever had.

Wally caught the smile. He touched her hand. "And another thing. Keep busy. Maybe your daughter don't need you as much as she did, but there must be other children who could do with a little attention. Not to mention some good home cooking. Am I right?"

She thought of Gus Pike. He always looked half starved to her eyes. Then there were those Mullin brats who lived down by the north shore. Their mother was ill, she'd heard, not able to look after them properly. Why, the littlest one, Maggie her name was, didn't even have a decent skirt to her name. Eulalie straightened up. She could stitch her up something in no time. Yes, and that beanpole of a farmhand, the one who worked for Archie Gillis, why, the bottom was out of his trousers. He was almost indecent. She'd noticed him the other day. He needed a warm sweater, too. He'd grown out of his old one. His wrists poked out of the ragged sleeves like the empty hands of a scarecrow. Her fingers itched for her knitting needles. She blew her nose and stood up.

"You're a good man, Wally Higgens. Thank you for that advice. I won't keep you any longer."

Wally jumped up. His feet felt like blocks of ice. "You'll be right as rain, very soon, poopsie," he assured her. "Or my name's not Wally Higgens."

"I believe I will. And it's thanks to you. I won't walk back with you to the boarding house, if you don't mind. I must get home. I've just realized I've a million and one things to do."

"I've got to get going too. I've a long journey and a busy day ahead of me." He raised his mushroom hat. "Goodbye now, Mrs. Whatever-Your-Name-Is. Take care of those bunions."

She giggled. "Just call me Mrs. X."

She dipped into her pocket and then held out her hand to him. As he reached to shake it, something glimmered in her palm. His heart skipped a beat. Looking at her quickly, he saw that her wet face was beaming.

"I found it near the pond." She smiled. "After I left you at the boarding house, I went back to look for it, because you seemed so miserable. I know how it feels to lose something precious."

Slowly, Wally lifted the ring from her outstretched hand. The stones winked up at him, bright as the morning, unharmed by their fall.

"How can I ever thank you, Mrs. X?"

"You've already thanked me, Mr. Higgens. You listened to my worries and woes. You helped me."

He had passed the pond and disappeared through Mrs. Biggins's door before she realized she was still clutching his handkerchief. She looked down at it. The initials W. H. were embroidered in one corner in a fine, feathery stitch. She recognized a mother's touch.

Tucking the sodden, crumpled ball into her purse, Mrs. Bugle wended her way home. Her step was light, her head held high. She would wash his handkerchief as soon as she could. No doubt Hetty King would have a forwarding address for him. She would fold it carefully and wrap it up and send it to him in a little box. She would enclose a note, too, thanking him once again. She would not have to mention her complete recovery from the shadowy life of a thief. He had understood that already.

Chapter Sixteen

Wally was late. Out of breath from running back from the pond, he paid Mrs. Biggins and tipped the boy for bringing Bumbles round from the stable. Of course he was delighted about the ring, yet, strangely enough, the conversation with Mrs. X had cheered him even more. Instead of feeling like the laughingstock of Avonlea, he now felt as though he had helped someone, done some good in the world. There was nothing quite like that feeling, he thought, lifting his sample cases onto the buggy. Like you had a little candle shining inside you, keeping you warm. Hmm. *The light that shines.The ties that bind.* For the first time in at least a week his mind tentatively flexed its muscles around a ditty.

He worked quickly, anxious to be gone. It was a shame, he thought, that such a pretty town would now forever be associated in his mind with his calamity. *Oh Hetty King. Of thee I sing. You lost my ring. Your neck I'll wring.*

"Wally Higgens!"

Hetty's voice came at him out of the blue, making him jump. He turned, reddening guiltily. He expected to see her waving an umbrella in his face, threatening to run him out of town for making up rude ditties. But she stood there meekly, looking up at him.

"I need to speak to you, Wally," she said more softly. It was not her usual, imperious tone; it was more like a plea.

Wally descended from the buggy slowly. This reluctance to face Hetty was new. It made him sad, for it contrasted sharply with the way he had felt when he'd first met her. Then, he had felt driven to see her every minute of the day. Whatever excuse he could dream up was enough. He would leap into his buggy and go chasing out to Rose Cottage, singing at the top of his voice. He had felt like a small boy skipping across fields. He had wanted to race and jump and lift his voice in song. Then had come the calamity, and his spirits had sunk so low that he had believed they would never, ever rise. But since his chat with Mrs. X, he had felt quite cheerful. He did not want to lose that cheerfulness. He did not want ever again to feel as sad as Hetty had once made him feel.

"There's nothing left to say, Miss King," he said now, forcing himself to look straight at her. "I saw the truth yesterday."

"The truth? What truth?"

"The truth of you and your betrothed, Wellington Campbell. I saw you kneeling there, holding him in your arms. I saw the truth in your face. It was true love."

An arrow of guilt pierced Hetty's heart. Wally was right. He had seen the truth in her face, only, being Wally, he had misinterpreted it. What he had seen in her face was grief. Grief over the terrible consequences her deceit had wrought on the people around her. She no more loved Wellington Campbell than she loved Wally Higgens. In fact, she had abused them both. She was sorry for what she had done. And that was why she had wept, as she knelt over her neighbor. But if she were to tell Wally the truth, would he not misinterpret that, too? Would he not assume that if she did not love Welly, then she must love Wally? She stood there, not knowing what to say.

"Things aren't always what they seem, Wally," she said finally, taking refuge in a cliché.

Wally struggled with the impulse to gaze one last time at her feet, those perfect tootsie-wootsies. "I would have fought like a tiger for you, sugar dumpling." He fixed his gaze on her hat, which, he saw now, had several plump red cherries swinging from it. "But I care too much for you to come between you and the man you love. I know when I'm beat." His eyes slipped downward involuntarily, but he yanked them back. "I'll withdraw that lawsuit, don't you worry."

"That is very gentlemanly of you, Wally. Very gentlemanly indeed."

To Hetty's amazement, she felt tears prick at the back of her eyes. She saw now that, despite his grammar and his loud ways, he was indeed a gentleman. A horrible doubt invaded her mind. Had she made a mistake? Could she perhaps have found happiness after all with this portly salesman from the Windy City?

She thought of the bustle and excitement he had brought to her quiet life. She thought of the presents, the compliments, the surprised, teasing comments of her relatives, the envious reaction of neighbors. How agreeable, she thought, to be courted, to be at the center of someone's life. But courting was one thing, marriage another. She saw that what she enjoyed was the attention and the knowledge that he liked her, liked her enough to want to spend the rest of his days with her. She was grateful to him for that. But she saw too that the glamour of his going away was clouding her judgment. In saying goodbye, he was removing himself from her, which made her immediately want to reach out and stop him. Were he to stay, she would lose interest immediately. Having recognized this foible of human nature in herself, she felt better.

Living alone was not something to be feared. The life she led—filled with friends, relatives, books—was one to be treasured. It was a rich, generous life. With sudden clarity she saw that she could be more fulfilled living by herself than she could ever be by marrying Wally and denying her own nature. No, she did not want to marry this man. But she did, at the very least, owe him the truth.

Reaching out, she took his hand. "I regret having done anything to hurt you, Wally," she said sincerely. "You're a warm, kind man and I like you very much. But I never said I loved you."

Wally shook the hand she offered. "Goodbye, poopsie. I'll write to you, just so you'll know where I am. But I don't expect to return."

Once safely seated on the buggy, he allowed his eyes a final treat. For one heavenly moment they lingered on Hetty's size six, quad A feet, neatly encased in shiny black boots. He sighed one long, last sigh. Then he sat bolt upright and adjusted his hat to an almost jaunty angle.

"Please keep the skates, Hetty King," he said, flicking the reins at Bumbles. "I wouldn't want anyone else in the world to wear them."

Hetty smiled at him. She watched him steer the buggy down the street, around the corner and out of her life. She would treasure those skates. Deep in her cedar-lined blanket box, she would store them, wrapped in soft cotton. From time to time she would remove them to wax and polish them. And as she did so, her nephews and nieces would gather round and she would recount once again the story of Wally Higgens and the calamity of his courting. In years to come they, in their turn, would relate the same story to their children.

Raising her gloved hand, she waved him farewell. "Goodbye," she called softly. "Bon voyage, poopsie!"

❧ ❧ ❧

Skylark takes you on the...

Road to Avonlea *

Based on the Sullivan Films production adapted from the novels of
LUCY MAUD MONTGOMERY

☐ THE JOURNEY BEGINS, Book #1 $3.99/NCR   48027-8

☐ THE STORY GIRL EARNS HER NAME, Book #2 $3.99/NCR   48028-6

☐ SONG OF THE NIGHT, Book #3 $3.99/NCR   48029-4

☐ THE MATERIALIZING OF DUNCAN McTAVISH, Book #4 $3.99/NCR   48030-8

☐ QUARANTINE AT ALEXANDER ABRAHAM'S, Book #5 $3.99/NCR   48031-6

☐ CONVERSATIONS, Book #6 $3.99/NCR   48032-4

☐ AUNT ABIGAIL'S BEAU, Book #7 $3.99/NCR   48033-2

☐ MALCOLM AND THE BABY, Book #8 $3.99/NCR   48034-0

☐ FELICITY'S CHALLENGE, Book #9 $3.99/NCR   48035-9

☐ THE HOPE CHEST OF ARABELLA KING, Book #10 $3.99/NCR   48036-7

☐ NOTHING ENDURES BUT CHANGE, Book #11 $3.99/NCR   48037-5

☐ SARA'S HOMECOMING, Book #12 $3.99/NCR   48038-3

☐ AUNT HETTY'S ORDEAL, Book #13 $3.99/NCR   48039-1

☐ OF CORSETS AND SECRETS AND TRUE, TRUE LOVE, Book #14 $3.99/NCR   48040-5

☐ OLD QUARRELS, OLD LOVE, Book #15 $3.99/NCR   48041-3

☐ FAMILY RIVALRY, #16 $3.99/NCR   48042-1

*ROAD TO AVONLEA is the trademark of Sullivan Films Inc.

BANTAM BOOKS
Dept. SK50, 2451 South Wolf Road, Des Plaines, IL 60018

Please send me the items I have checked above. I am enclosing
$_____ (please add $2.50 to cover postage and handling).
Send check or money order, no cash or C.O.D.'s please.

MR/MS _____

ADDRESS _____

CITY/STATE _____ ZIP _____

Please allow four to six weeks for delivery.
Prices and availability subject to change without notice.   SK50-8/93